Abigail

The Amish of Morrissey County Book Three

Sylvia Price

Penn and Ink Writing, LLC

Stay Up to Date with Sylvia Price

Subscribe to Sylvia's newsletter at newsletter.sylviaprice.com to get to know Sylvia and her family. It's also a great way to stay in the loop about new releases, freebies, promos, and more.

As a thank-you, you will receive several FREE exclusive short stories that aren't available for purchase.

Porsche's
INTUITION
A Jonah's Redemption Story
SYLVIA PRICE

HOPE
for Hannah's
LOVE
Amish Love Through the Seasons
SHORT STORY
SYLVIA PRICE

SYLVIA PRICE
EVE
AN ELIJAH COMPANION STORY

Praise for Sylvia Price's Books

"Author Sylvia Price wrote a storyline that enthralled me. The characters are unique in their own way, which made it more interesting. I highly recommend reading this book. I'll be reading more of Author Sylvia Price's books."

"You can see the love of the main characters and the love that the author has for the main characters and her writing. This book is so wonderful. I cannot wait to read more from this beautiful writer."

"The storyline caught my attention from the very beginning and kept me interested throughout the entire book. I loved the chemistry between the characters."

"A wonderful, sweet and clean story with strong characters. Now I just need to know what happens next!"

"First time reading this author, and I'm very impressed! I love feeling the godliness of this story."

"This was a wonderful story that reminded me of a glorious God we have."

"I encourage all to read this uplifting story of faith and friendship."

"I love Sylvia's books because they are filled with love and faith."

Other Books by Sylvia Price

Jonah's Redemption: Book 1 – FREE

Jonah's Redemption: Book 2 – http://getbook.at/jonah2

Jonah's Redemption: Book 3 – http://getbook.at/jonah3

Jonah's Redemption: Book 4 – http://getbook.at/jonah4

Jonah's Redemption: Book 5 – http://getbook.at/jonah5

Jonah's Redemption: Boxed Set – http://getbook.at/jonahset

The Christmas Arrival – http://getbook.at/christmasarrival

Seeds of Spring Love (Amish Love Through the Seasons Book 1) – http://getbook.at/seedsofspring

Sprouts of Summer Love (Amish Love Through the Seasons Book 2) – http://getbook.at/

sproutsofsummer
Fruits of Fall Love (Amish Love Through the Seasons Book 3) – http://getbook.at/fruitsoffall
Waiting for Winter Love (Amish Love Through the Seasons Book 4) – http://getbook.at/waitingforwinter
Amish Love Through the Seasons Boxed Set (The Complete Series) – http://getbook.at/amishseasons

Elijah: An Amish Story of Crime and Romance – http://getbook.at/elijah

The Christmas Cards – http://getbook.at/christmascards

A Promised Tomorrow (The Yoder Family Saga Prequel) – FREE
Peace for Yesterday (The Yoder Family Saga Book 1) – http://getbook.at/peaceforyesterday
A Path for Tomorrow (The Yoder Family Saga Book 2) – http://getbook.at/pathfortomorrow
Faith for the Future (The Yoder Family Saga Book 3) – http://getbook.at/faithforthefuture
Patience for the Present (The Yoder Family Saga Book 4) – http://getbook.at/patienceforthepresent

Return to Yesterday (The Yoder Family Saga Book 5) – http://getbook.at/returntoyesterday
The Yoder Family Saga Boxed Set (The Complete Series) – http://getbook.at/yoderbox

The Origins of Cardinal Hill (The Amish of Cardinal Hill Prequel) – FREE
The Beekeeper's Calendar (The Amish of Cardinal Hill Book 1) – http://getbook.at/beekeeperscalendar
The Soapmaker's Recipe (The Amish of Cardinal Hill Book 2) – http://getbook.at/soapmakersrecipe
The Herbalist's Remedy (The Amish of Cardinal Hill Book 3) – http://getbook.at/herbalistsremedy

Sarah (The Amish of Morrissey County Prequel) – FREE
Sadie (The Amish of Morrissey County Book 1) – http://getbook.at/sadie
Bridget (The Amish of Morrissey County Book 2) – http://getbook.at/bridget
Abigail (The Amish of Morrissey County Book 3) – http://getbook.at/morrisseyabigail
Eliza (The Amish of Morrissey County Book 4) – http://getbook.at/eliza
Dorothy (The Amish of Morrissey County

Book 5) – http://getbook.at/dorothy

Songbird Cottage Beginnings (Pleasant Bay Prequel) – FREE
The Songbird Cottage (Pleasant Bay Book 1) – http://getbook.at/songbirdcottage
Return to Songbird Cottage (Pleasant Bay Book 2) – http://getbook.at/returntosongbird
Escape to Songbird Cottage (Pleasant Bay Book 3) – http://getbook.at/escapetosongbird
Secrets of Songbird Cottage (Pleasant Bay Book 4) – http://getbook.at/secretsofsongbird
Seasons at Songbird Cottage (Pleasant Bay Book 5) – http://getbook.at/seasonsatsongbird
The Songbird Cottage Boxed Set (Pleasant Bay Complete Series Collection) – http://getbook.at/songbirdbox

The Crystal Crescent Inn (Sambro Lighthouse Book 1) – http://getbook.at/cci1
The Crystal Crescent Inn (Sambro Lighthouse Book 2) – http://getbook.at/cci2
The Crystal Crescent Inn (Sambro Lighthouse Book 3) – http://getbook.at/cci3
The Crystal Crescent Inn (Sambro Lighthouse Book 4) – http://getbook.at/cci4

The Crystal Crescent Inn (Sambro Lighthouse Book 5) – http://getbook.at/cci5
The Crystal Crescent Inn Boxed Set (Sambro Lighthouse Complete Series Collection) – http://getbook.at/ccibox

Contents

Unofficial Glossary of Pennsylvania Dutch Words

Ach – Oh

Amisch – Amish

Boppli – baby

Brieder – brothers

Bu/buwe – boy(s)

Daed – dad

Danki – thanks

Dochder – daughter

Eldre – parents

Englisch/Englischer – non-Amish person

Familye – family

Fraa – wife

Gmay – local Amish community

Gott – God

Groossdaadi – grandfather

Groossmaami – grandmother

Gude daag – Hello (literally Good day)

Gude naamidaag – Good afternoon

Gude nacht – Good night

Gut – good

Kapp – Amish head covering

Kinner – children

Kossin – cousin

Kumm – come

Liewer/Liewi– dear (male/female)

Mach's gut – Make it good (a parting phrase)

Maedel/maed – girl(s)

Maem – mom

Mann – husband/man

Nee – no

Nochber – neighbor(s)

Ordnung – the written and unwritten rules of the Amish

Rumspringa – running around period for Amish youth

Sing – a Sunday evening social gathering of Amish youth

Soh – son

Ya – yes

Chapter One

1980
Morrissey County, Pennsylvania

A smile curved Jonas Smoker's lips as he bent over and tenderly touched the tiny sprout of corn that had made its way up out of the newly planted ground. Straightening, he closed his eyes and took in a deep breath of the fresh spring air.

"Surely, this is what life is all about, *Gott*," Jonas whispered into the stillness of the afternoon. When he was outside working by himself, he felt closer to the Lord than He ever did in any church service.

Heading east toward the house, where he knew that his mother, Barbara, was waiting with a fresh pitcher of cold lemonade, Jonas considered how much their little family endured over the last few years and just how far they had come. His family had faced the real fear of losing their farm and all they had when his father passed away, but the Lord was faithful and worked through Jonas's efforts to save their property. It had taken a lot of hard work, many sleepless nights, and countless prayers being raised to the Lord in heaven, but things were finally headed in the right direction.

Now the farm was thriving. Jonas was expanding production to facilitate yielding double the wheat crop and had also looked into having someone come to bale hay in the back fields; Jonas planned to keep part of the harvest to feed their animals over winter, while the rest of it would be sold to other local farmers without the capacity to bale their own.

Striding toward the house, Jonas's gaze traveled toward the barn, where he had been working to build pens for calves. With what little money he managed to save, he had already determined that he would buy two or three dozen bottle calves to raise to adulthood and then sell. The money he earned from them would in turn be sown right back into future calf purchases and ultimately to expand the barn.

Jonas was doing everything in his power to ensure that the Smoker homestead would flourish to its full potential, yielding crops and animal produce of the highest quality that would be sought after by many. The Lord had blessed Jonas beyond his wildest dreams, and he was determined to do everything in his power to be faithful with what he had, meet his family's needs, and provide for others, too. Being a shrewd businessman and making the most of his blessings so that they would double or triple in returns was a wise investment, and it honored the Lord.

Jonas pushed open the back door and stepped inside, turning once again to take another look at the crops in the fields.

"*Ach*, what a beautiful morning *Gott* has given us!" Jonas exclaimed as he made his way to the kitchen. Stopping in front of the wash basin, he began to scrub the dirt off his hands. He wasn't sure what to make of the expression on his mother's face when he met her gaze. She seemed almost disheartened as she began to mold dough into loaves of bread and arrange them on the kitchen table.

"*Ya*, I suppose so," Barbara muttered as she gave a loaf of bread a final pat. "Do you want something to drink?"

Nodding, Jonas grinned and said, "You always manage to read my mind. I'd love some of your delicious lemonade."

Although Barbara smiled, it seemed strained. Pulling out a pitcher of lemonade from the icebox, she commented, "I noticed you didn't go to the *sing* last night. I thought you were planning on making it this time."

Jonas groaned inwardly and desperately hoped that his mien and body language wouldn't betray the truth of how frustrated her words were making him. Initially, when Jonas stopped going to young peoples' events after the death of his father, Barbara had been understanding. But now it seemed that with each week that passed with him not attending social events, she was becoming more obsessed with him missing the chance at meeting his mate.

Shrugging, Jonas accepted the proffered glass of lemonade and said, "*Ach*, I'm not worried about *sings*. I hardly have time to think about going out with a bunch of foolish teenagers and having fun. I am much too busy working here on the farm—by the time Sunday comes around, I just want to stay home and rest."

Barbara met his gaze with eyes that appeared almost red as she somberly asked, "But Jonas, how do you ever expect to find a *fraa* if you don't get out of the house?"

A wife. So that's what has her so upset. The mere thought of being pressured to find a wife made Jonas feel sick to his stomach, and he wished that he could both convey to his mother and make her understand exactly how he felt. He had never been one to concern himself with romance and the like, and after taking on the responsibilities of the farm, he quickly discovered that hard work could replace any feeling of emptiness his heart might harbor. Besides, their family had already suffered enough loss. Why add more people to it who ultimately might be lost as well?

Chuckling softly, Jonas tried to communicate how unfazed and blasé he was about the prospect of finding a wife as he announced, "Aww, *Maem.* I wish you'd stop worrying about me finding a *fraa!* You were never one to try to push me out into the world or try to convince me to find a *maedel.*"

"Of course not!" Barbara countered as she grabbed a dishrag and wiped some lemonade off the side of the pitcher. "But that was when you were just a young *bu.* You're an adult now, Jonas— an adult with a life ahead of you."

Nodding in agreement, Jonas took a sip of his drink before saying, "*Ya,* a life that is plenty full already. I have this entire farm to try to work and make a success. I've already managed to do so much just in the last few years." Raising an eyebrow, he added, "How far would I have gotten if I'd had my mind on *maed* and trying to find someone to court?"

Reaching out to grab her son's arm, a discernable desperation glinted in Barbara's eyes as she urged, "*Soh*, you have done remarkable things with the farm; it's true. But I can't help but think that *Gott* has a lot more in store for your life than just this. You know the way of the Bible and of our culture—it's to marry and to raise a *familye*. Don't you want to have someone to continue your legacy on this farm when you pass away? Do you want it to just be auctioned off to strangers?"

Trying not to roll his eyes at her grave argument for having a family, Jonas stated, "*Maem*, I appreciate your concern, but I'm not too worried about what will happen after I die. The Lord has given me this property, and He wants me to put it to *gut* use. I intend to do just that—even if it is to be the focus of everything I do. As far as saying it's *Gott's* way to get married and have *kinner*—well, seems to me that the Apostle Paul had plenty to say about the benefits of remaining single. Besides, look at Jesus Himself! Jesus never married, and He accomplished the greatest of things for *Gott's* kingdom."

Rather than her son's words striking a chord in her, Barbara appeared to become more exasperated and distressed. Throwing her hands up to emphasize her point, she exclaimed, "Jonas! You're not Jesus, for sure, and I want you to remember what awaited Paul in his singleness—a life that was riddled with being persecuted and imprisoned for his faith. At least his faith was expressed by his works, not simply making his land his sole pursuit." Sighing deeply, she added, "A *fraa* would help you to reorganize your priorities and to understand there is so much more to life than trying to be successful and working your life away."

"*Ya*," Jonas shot back before he could even think better of it, "I suppose I could do what you did and marry, only to spend the rest of my life grieving and miserable. Since *Daed* died, you have done nothing but wallow in misery. I don't know why you'd want a similar life for me."

Jonas instantly regretted his words, and the expression on his mother's face only added to it. While he had spoken truth, it was not in love or seasoned with grace; his mother looked at him like he had plunged a knife right through her. She sucked in a deep breath of air and worked to compose herself.

"I'm sorry, *Maem*—" Jonas started to say.

Barbara, holding up a hand, interjected, "I just want you to find someone you can love and enjoy spending the rest of your life with. I want you to know the joy of feeling your heart skip when you see the *fraa* you love heading toward you. I want you to feel the surge of overwhelming wonder when your firstborn *boppli* is placed in your arms. I want you to be able to know what it's like to share everything with someone. *Ya*, you're right, I have been miserable since your *daed* died. But not because I regret my choices. Rather, I am still grieving what I have lost. Your *daed* was more than just my *mann*—he was a part of me. Like *Gott* says, the two of us had 'become one flesh,' and losing him has been like losing a chunk of myself."

Barbara turned to put her bread in the oven. Jonas stood watching, wishing he knew the words to say that might be able to ease the tension between them. The silence was palpable, and he felt overwhelmed with awkwardness.

Shaking his head to clear his thoughts, Jonas

mumbled, "I'm going back out to the barn."

Barbara didn't say anything in reply, and Jonas didn't wait for her to speak; instead, he started out toward the barn without another word. He was anxious to get his mind back on work and off of the words recently exchanged with his mother.

Jonas didn't have time in his life or room in his heart for a woman, no matter what his mother might have to say about the joys, delights, and rewards of marriage. His vision was focused entirely on farming and making a success of his father's dream. If Jonas stuck with it, he knew that he would be able to fulfill all that his father had once envisioned for the property.

There was no time to think about anything else. Jonas was going to stick to the path set out before him and thank the Lord for all that he'd been given. If his mother wanted to worry about romance, then she was simply going to have to look for someone else to play matchmaker for because Jonas was determined that he was going to spend the rest of his life alone. He wouldn't ever risk becoming a lonely widower with a broken heart!

Chapter Two

bigail Speicher couldn't help but think that the ride on the hard buggy seat was the most uncomfortable one of her life. While she was used to the hard wooden seats of Amish buggies, this particular ride was so horrifically boring that there was nothing to distract her from her discomfort.

"I built that fence right there," her riding companion, Pete Zook, announced as he pointed toward a black plank fence that ran alongside the road. Whistling to himself, he smiled broadly as he explained, "That one right there earned me a right pretty penny...along with being called the best fence builder in all of Morrissey County."

Biting down on her bottom lip, Abigail tried to keep her negative comeback to herself. She and Pete had not known each other well before that day, but when he asked her to go on a buggy ride with him, her mother encouraged her to say yes. Now Abigail was beginning to wonder what exactly possessed her to agree. If she'd spent even a few minutes around Pete in the past, surely she would have recognized that he was one of the most boring, self-absorbed young men in the community.

"*Ya*, I do a lot of work," Pete continued as he pushed his black felt hat a little higher up on his forehead and looked at her. Dripping with pride, he added, "I do work, and I do it well." Puffing out his chest, he bragged, "Some people say that I'm set to be the most successful young man in our entire *gmay*. I wouldn't be surprised if that really does happen. My work lasts. If you talk to most people, they have complaints about the things that carpenters build for them. Not my clients. The people I work for have nothing to offer but compliments about my work. Not to mention, I'm one of Bishop Abron Kauffman's favorite *nochber*. When he has a problem, I'm the one he calls. And you know how particular the bishop is...but he's never had a complaint about me."

Pointing toward a barn in the distance, Pete added, "I built that barn, too. It was one of my favorite projects to work on. The owner of that property told me that he could hardly believe I knew so much, being as young as I am."

Abigail squinted at the barn in the distance. Little did Pete know that the barn belonged to her second cousin. And, while it was a well-made building, it in fact had quite a few flaws. Not long after its construction, the foundation needed work, and someone had been called in from out of town to fix the original mistakes.

Shrugging, Abigail decided not to answer Pete one way or the other. Instead, she just stared at the trees at the side of the road and let her mind wander. If Pete could be so far off about that barn, was there any truth to any of the stories that he had told her? Was he even an adequate carpenter, never mind a proficient one? His need to brag made Abigail wonder if anything he had told her wasn't exaggerated and embellished.

Abigail began to work her hands together as they lay in her lap. They had been riding for almost an hour, and Pete had yet to even ask her anything about herself! While Abigail was somewhat relieved in not having to talk, she found it annoying that he showed so little interest in anyone other than himself. Her only hope was that they would soon get back to the Speicher homestead and that Pete would choose to leave. Fear that her mother might invite him to stay for supper washed over Abigail, and she prayed fervently that the Lord would protect her from such a horrific event.

Abigail glanced at Pete, who was still talking non-stop. It seemed that the man hardly stopped talking long enough to even take a breath of air! Sighing deeply, she tried not to let her inner dissatisfaction show. After all, Pete might be the only option that she had left.

Letting her mind travel back to her courting years, Abigail pondered whether there was someone else that she could have missed as a possible match. They did, after all, live in a large community. How had it turned out that she was one of the few girls who was left with no boyfriend to drive her home from *sings* or plan a future alongside?

Listening to Pete ramble on, Abigail silently admitted that she would be more than happy to stay single forever if her options were limited to dealing with the likes of him.

"Abigail! Abigail!" The sound of someone calling her drew her surprised and relieved attention, and she smiled when she recognized her cousin in the distance. Walking directly toward them, Susan Black was waving frantically, urging them to slow down.

Reaching out to grab the reins, Abigail said, "*Ach*, Pete! Stop. There's my *kossin*."

Pulling back on the reins, Pete pulled the buggy to a halt. Before he could act, Abigail jumped down from the buggy and hurried to her cousin's side. Throwing her arms around Susan, Abigail hugged her tightly and whispered against her ear, "Save me!"

Grabbing Susan's arm as she stepped back, Abigail glanced up at the buggy and called out, "*Danki* for the ride, Pete. Sorry I had to cut it short."

Abigail didn't give Pete time to try to stop her. Instead, she just started down the road, side by side with Susan, clinging to her cousin's arm for dear life.

"Don't look back!" Abigail said between clenched teeth as she picked up her pace. "Just keep going, and let's get away from him as quickly as possible."

Susan began to laugh, covering her audible giggles with a hand. Finally collecting herself, she asked, "Is this a date that went badly?"

Rolling her eyes, Abigail shook her head and

said, "You have no idea, *Kossin*. It has been nothing short of a nightmare." Trying to distract herself from the terrible memories of the ride she had just endured, she said, "But let's not talk about that. What brings you to Morrissey County?"

Shaking her head, Susan said, "*Ach*, Andrew had to *kumm* here to see his *groossdaadi*, and I decided to walk out to your house to see if you all were home while he finishes up his visit. He plans to stop by and get me on his way home."

Giving her cousin a sideways glance, Abigail asked, "Is marriage as *gut* as you hoped?"

"Even better!" Susan assured her. Placing a hand on her expanding stomach, she grinned broadly and said, "And it seems like *Gott* has a new role ready for me here soon. We're expecting our first *boppli* this fall."

Oohing in delight, Abigail clapped her hands together and said, "I'm so happy for you! If it's a *maedel*, you'll have to name her after me."

The conversation grew somewhat more cheerful as Susan began to tell stories about her new life out of Morrissey County with her husband. However, as Susan talked, Abigail felt a sense of sadness taint the enjoyable atmosphere. Knowing how happy her cousin was made Abigail glad for her yet somewhat sorry for herself. Was there any chance that she would ever have a future with a husband of her own? That she would ever get to carry a child and then deliver it, helping to raise it up within their community?

As if she could read her mind, Susan asked, "Have you had any hopes of a *mann* in your future?"

Raising an eyebrow, Abigail looked at her a little scornfully as she said, "I'm sure you know the answer to that one, considering the ride I just managed to escape."

Laughing again, Susan wove her arm through Abigail's and said, "Don't despair, my dear *kossin*. I'm sure that *Gott* has something *gut* in store for your future."

Yet, even as Abigail listened to the words she longed to hold onto, she found them as elusive as trying to grasp hold of an apple in water. It was starting to seem that the Lord might just intend for her to be alone for the rest of her life.

When the Speicher house came into view, Abigail grimaced at the sight of a buggy parked next to the porch. Her mother was outside, talking to the driver. Even from a distance, the two girls could hear the driver of the buggy ranting, and

Abigail quickly recognized him as none other than Pete Zook himself.

Frowning, she had to make a conscious effort to keep herself from turning and running in the other direction.

"I tried my best!" Pete declared with a disgusted tone. "I took her out on a ride. I tried to have a *gut* time with her...but she was totally rude to me! Before I even knew what had happened, she jumped down off my buggy and took off. If this is the way that your *dochder* treats her potential suitors, then it's no surprise that she is still single. I was just trying to do you all a favor. I know you're not doing too *gut* health-wise, and I thought that I'd make sure that she didn't end up all alone. Well, that's a mistake I won't make again! I will not take her out ever again. At least not until she offers me a formal apology and treats me with more respect. For pity's sake, my *eldre* are friends with the bishop...how do you think Abron Kauffman will feel about this?"

Sucking in a deep breath, Abigail wrestled to keep her anger in check. Surely, it would do no good to go up to the house while Pete was there talking to her mother.

Glancing at Abigail out of the corner of

her eye, Susan seemed to be assessing Abigail's reaction. Squeezing her cousin's elbow, Susan whispered, "*Ach*, Abigail. Don't pay any attention to him. I'm sure that your *maem* will understand why you didn't want to ride with him."

But Abigail wasn't so sure at all. Her mother had become so consumed with ensuring that her youngest daughter got married that she was probably unwilling to turn down any potential suitor, even someone as disgusting as Pete.

Finally, Pete urged his horse to move down the drive, and Colette retreated back into the house. Watching her mother's thin frame take refuge in their farmhouse, Abigail's heart ached within her chest. How she wished that she could make her mother's biggest dream come true.

When Pete drove past them, he didn't even raise a hand or speak. Instead, he just bored into Abigail with a cold, icy stare.

"How about you stay outside for a minute?" Abigail suggested as she and Susan reached the porch.

Nodding, Susan took a seat in one of the hardwood chairs, allowing Abigail to go in and talk to her mother alone.

Just as Abigail had feared, Colette was seated

by the empty fireplace. She had her Bible spread open on her lap, but the elderly woman wasn't reading it. Instead, her hands covered her face, and her shoulders were shaking.

"*Maem.*" Abigail shook her head sadly as she went to her mother's side and put a hand on her thin shoulder. "*Maem*…I'm sorry." She couldn't think of anything else to say.

Looking up at her daughter, tears streamed down Colette's sallow cheeks as she whispered, "Why? Why, Abigail? Don't you know how hard I am trying to hold onto hope? It is my greatest dream that *Gott* will provide you with a *mann* before I die." Letting out a moan, she whispered, "I was so blessed to receive a surprise *boppli* so late in life…but now I'm afraid that you will be all alone once I pass away."

Abigail couldn't bear to think of her mother dying. Not only did thoughts of her death fill Abigail with a deep loneliness, but they also stirred up an intense fear. What would she do once Colette passed away? It was hard to know. Abigail knew that she wouldn't be left alone to enjoy the large homestead by herself. Instead, it would likely be sold to pay off debts, and Abigail would be expected to go stay with one of her married siblings in a different state. Everything that she loved about her family's farm and the small farm supply store that they ran from the front of their property would likely be lost as Abigail was tossed around like an unwanted stray cat.

Yet, even that fate seemed better than being forced to live a lifetime with someone like Pete Zook. Swallowing hard, Abigail's voice grew soft as she whispered, "I'm sorry, *Maem*. I just couldn't stand being with him. You have to see that. Surely, you do. He was only interested in himself. I couldn't bear the thought of being married to someone like that!"

Nodding, Colette wiped at her eyes as she admitted, "I'm not upset with you, *Liewi*. I'm just upset that things have turned out this way. I was so hopeful that Pete would be the right match for you."

Pulling herself to her feet, Colette reached out and gathered Abigail up against her in a hug. Holding her tightly, Colette whispered, "I guess I will just keep on praying."

Trying to distract her mother, Abigail suggested that they go out on the porch to visit with Susan. Surely, seeing their sweet relative would help Colette to feel better. And Abigail determined that she would pray that *Gott* would open a door so that it would be possible for her to fulfill her mother's last and greatest dream.

Chapter Three

Jonas nailed another piece of wood in place. If he was going to have this barn ready for the load of calves that he was set to have delivered within the next two weeks, he was going to have to work extra hard and tirelessly. Pulling himself up straighter, he groaned as he massaged a sore muscle in his lower back. Reaching for his bucket of nails, he let out another groan when he realized how low his supply was getting.

Jonas always sourced his building supplies in town. The idea of taking the time required for the long trip to the store seemed frustrating. Unless he wanted to spend an hour or so on the road, he would need to hire a driver. And finding an *Englisch* driver who was available to give him a ride could be a time-consuming endeavor.

Frowning in thought, Jonas considered the Speichers' supply store. He hadn't been there since

Amos Speicher passed away. He wondered if the store was even still open. Jonas's father had always gone there to make his purchases, determined that it was best to buy supplies from someone right there within their community.

"*Ach*," Jonas muttered to himself, "I guess it's worth a try."

While he wasn't sure what state the Speichers' store would be in, he supposed that it would be better to make the short twenty-minute ride there before he tried to tackle the long drive into town.

Going to the horse stall, Jonas called for one of the horses and motioned for it to come to his side. It was time to hitch up and see what the Speicher family might have to offer.

By the dim light of the supply store, Abigail lifted some boards of wood and arranged them on one of the shelves. When her father had passed away two years prior, she and her mother discussed shutting the store down completely, but it seemed sad to put an end to her father's biggest dream. Running the store was always such a joy to him, and he had considered it to be the best way to serve the community.

While Colette typically ran the store, today she was lying down inside while Abigail restocked the dwindling items on the shelves. It was hard work, and she was glad that her mother had agreed to stay inside rather than try to help.

While working alone, Abigail had secretly been considering the possibility of asking to stay there on the homestead once her mother passed away. If she could work in the supply store and make a success of it, perhaps her brothers and sisters would give her a chance. Though considering their low customer turnout, it seemed unlikely that would be a possibility.

A knock on the side door made her stand to attention, and Abigail reached to push some of her hair back under her prayer *kapp*.

"*Kumm* in!" Abigail called out cheerily. It would be the first customer all day.

The door swung open, and a young man stepped into the building. Abigail's gaze narrowed as she tried to work out if she recognized him.

"*Gude daag.* Do you have any nails in stock?" the deep but jovial voice asked.

Nodding, Abigail rubbed her hands on her black apron as she headed toward the front of the store to greet the customer. She instantly felt her interest piqued when the unfamiliar young Amish man came into view. He was tall and strong with muscular arms and a broad smile.

"We have nails…right over here," Abigail told him, leading him toward the area of the store where the nails were kept.

"You've got quite a nice store here," he commented, his eyes trailing the shelves as he followed her across the building.

Nodding to show her appreciation, Abigail smiled and said, "*Ya*, we try to keep it that way. Ever since my *daed* passed away, it's been hard to keep everything in stock and advertise…but we're trying our best."

Stopping beside the nails, Abigail lifted a hand and laid it on the selection as she explained, "As you can see, we have a lot of different sized nails available."

"*Ya*, this is perfect," he said as he reached out for one of the boxes of nails. "I'm working on getting our barn ready for new calves, so I ought to be able to give you plenty of business."

Curiosity bubbled in Abigail. *Who is this*

handsome young man? Why have I never seen him before? Surely, he must already be married, or I would remember him from the sings.

"Do you and your *fraa* raise a lot of calves?" Abigail asked, trying to sound inconspicuous with her line of questioning.

Shaking his head, the young stranger smirked as he said, "It's me and my *maem*…although she generally stays inside the house. But, *nee*, this is our first year raising calves. Hopefully the first of many."

A flutter of hope surged through Abigail's chest. *He isn't married? How can this be?* She wanted to ask him outright but bit her tongue to keep at least an air of sensibility about herself.

"Sounds like a lot of work for one *mann*," Abigail commented.

"*Ya.*" He nodded. "But it's all right. I like the work. The farm is my entire life." As he set the nails down on the counter, he surprised Abigail by offering his hand and saying, "I'm Jonas Smoker."

Jonas Smoker. The name seemed completely unfamiliar to her.

Frowning, Abigail tried not to seem too interested as she admitted, "I don't think I've seen you at any of the young people's gatherings before."

Shaking his head, Jonas Smoker grinned as he admitted, "*Nee*, you wouldn't have seen me at one of those events. I'm not much of one for the *sings*. I'm afraid the farm keeps me too busy for that kind of fun."

There was undeniably a spark between them that was impossible for Abigail to ignore. It was the first time that she had ever come across a young man who actually seemed interesting to her *and* who seemed to show an interest in her by being more than happy to talk to her rather than rushing to get going. Could this young man possibly be the answer to her and her mother's prayers?

Jonas felt strangely clumsy and almost not himself standing next to the pretty worker at the supply store. He was so used to being focused on the farm that it had been years since he even attempted a conversation with a young woman.

"What's your name?" Jonas asked, noticing a pretty twinge of color flush her cheeks as he asked the question.

Shifting her weight from one foot to the other, she smiled a pretty smile as she looked up at him and handed him a handwritten receipt.

"I'm Abigail Speicher," she told him as he took the paper from her hands along with a few pieces of change.

Unsure where the question came from, Jonas found himself asking, "Does your *mann* own this place? I know you said that your *daed* owned it in the past."

"*Nee*," Abigail hurried to assure him with a shake of her head. "I'm not married. It's just my *maem* and me, too."

How ironic that she and I are living such similar lives! And, in some strange way, it was an incredible relief knowing that she didn't have a husband. *There's something about Abigail ...* Even as the thought flittered through his mind, Jonas worked to push it away.

Holding up the bag of nails, he smiled as he said, "Well, *danki* for the supplies. I'm sure I'll be back soon." Starting for the door, he turned back around and asked, "I don't suppose you know of any *Amisch* young men that are looking for a job, do you?"

Abigail scrunched her face up in a frown as she shook her head and replied, "None that I can think of."

Shrugging his shoulders, Jonas assured her, "No worries. I was just thinking that maybe you knew of someone who could help me get my barn ready for the calves. It's a big job, and my *maem* certainly isn't up to helping me with it. I have some friends, but their skills aren't the best. Well, if you think of anybody, just send them out to the Smoker farm. We're about twenty minutes from here."

Abigail's face broke out into a lovely smile as she promised him, "I'll be sure to do just that. I hope you remember our store when you need more supplies."

"That I can promise you!" Jonas said as he made his way out of the shed and into the spring day's fresh sunshine.

Climbing up into his buggy and placing the nails in the back seat, Jonas turned and glanced back at the store. Somewhere deep inside, he hoped that he would manage to catch another glimpse at the pretty little storekeeper. Unfortunately, it was not to be so. Shaking his head, he chastised himself for his disappointment.

"What's wrong with you, Jonas?" he chided as he urged his horse down the drive and towards the road. He had never been one to let a beautiful girl turn his head! So what had happened to him now? Shaking his head at his silliness, he forced himself to refocus on his plans to work on the barn as soon as he got home. He had a lot of work ahead of him, and he certainly didn't have time to start daydreaming about girls now!

Snorting at the crazy connection he felt with Abigail, he told himself that his mother must have gotten in his head more than he realized. He was going to have to simply put Abigail out of his mind. The next time he needed supplies, he would have to try and gauge when her mother might be working so he could avoid the pretty young girl and the temptation she represented.

Humming softly, Abigail put the finishing touches on the cake and then set it on the table. She had worked in the shop all afternoon but came inside at five o'clock to eat leftovers. Despite having a busy day of work, she felt so lighthearted that she hardly recognized her disposition.

"You sure seem to be in a *gut* mood today!" Colette spoke aloud the words that Abigail had just been thinking. Smiling at her daughter, she took a seat at the table and waited for the cake to be finished. "I guess working in the shop must do something *gut* for your spirits."

A smile tugged at the corners of Abigail's lips, and she shrugged. She didn't want to be too obvious, but it was hard to hide her feelings.

"I feel like I accomplished a lot," Abigail explained as she moved the cake to the table and then began pulling plates out of the cabinet on the wall. "You know I always enjoyed helping *Daed* build things…and I like to work in the store."

Sighing deeply, Colette got a faraway look in her eyes as she nodded and admitted, "*Ya*, I remember when we built this place. You were just a little *maedel*, not even out of school, yet you dug right in and helped your *daed* every step of the way. He told me that you were actually a better carpenter than your *brieder*."

The mention of her father brought bittersweet memories to mind. How she missed him at times!

"He wanted so badly to make a *gut* go of that shop," Colette said with a sigh as she shook her head. "But I don't know that it's going to work. Did you have any customers today?"

Shaking her own head, Abigail admitted, "I only had one. He came for a box of nails."

Images of Jonas Smoker filled her thoughts, and Abigail felt her face growing warm all over again. Forcing herself to push through her discomfort, she asked, "Do you know Jonas Smoker, *Maem*? He's the one who came into the shop. He's not very old, but I've not seen him before. He must be from the other *gmay*...but he says he doesn't go to the *sings*. I guess that's why he's a stranger."

Scrunching her face up into a frown, Colette took the piece of cake that Abigail presented and appeared to be deep in thought. Finally, she nodded her head and exclaimed, "*Ach, ya*! That would be Barbara's *bu*. Barbara Smoker lives right over the line in the other *gmay*. She's a *gut fraa*... lost her *mann* not too long ago. I've often thought that if I was in better health, I should go visit her. We seem to have a lot in common."

Abigail sat down across from her mother and listened intently. Even though she was holding a fork in her hand, it hovered above her cake, her ears tuned in to any word that Colette might say.

"I've heard that Jonas is a *gut bu*," Colette finally replied. Looking up at Abigail with a gaze that seemed to look right through her daughter, she knowingly added, "Unfortunately, he doesn't seem to be one that pays any mind to *maed*. His mother is worried sick that he'll never get married. He's a confirmed bachelor it seems."

While her mother seemed to be certain that was the final verdict, Abigail didn't let it bother or deter her. Shrugging, she took a bite of her cake and said, "He's needing some help out at his barn. I figured I might go by there tomorrow and see if I can lend a hand."

Colette's eyebrows rose a few inches, and she stared at Abigail as if she had grown another head. She opened her mouth to say something but then shut it quickly. Finally, just giving a nod, she said, "Whatever you want to do, *Liewi*."

Abigail smiled as she enjoyed the softness of the sweet chocolate cake. She was glad that her mother hadn't tried to convince her that seeing Jonas was a waste of her time. While Jonas Smoker might be a confirmed old bachelor in the making, Abigail wanted to at least try her hand at breaking down the guard that he had built around his heart. Perhaps it was God Himself who had brought the two of them together in the store earlier that day. Either way, Abigail was going to see for herself.

Chapter Four

Jonas tilted his head one way and then the other as he assessed the half-constructed calf pen. There was something about its craftsmanship that left a good deal to be desired! He had the muscle to do the work, but he was starting to wonder if he lacked the know-how to actually make his dream for the calf pens materialize into reality.

Sighing dejectedly at his project, Jonas wondered if it would really matter if the pen seemed to lean a little to the left. Frowning, he put his hand to his chin and scratched it slowly.

"Looks like you could use a level!" A woman's voice made Jonas turn around in surprise. It wasn't the voice of his mother, and Jonas certainly wasn't used to hearing other women's voices around the Smoker homestead.

Jonas couldn't have been more surprised to see

a young Amish girl standing in the barn behind him, her thin arms crossed against her chest and a happy smile on her lips. Instant recognition flooded Jonas's mind.

"Abigail Speicher." He said her name in amazement. "From the store."

Abigail nodded her head and smiled wider.

Although Jonas managed to grasp who had come to visit him, the real question was why. What on earth had possessed the total stranger to make her way out to his farm? How did she even know where he lived?

Taking a step forward on the hard-packed dirt barn floor, Abigail seemed to be trying to weigh the situation before saying anything else. Looking Jonas over, she finally admitted, "I guess you're probably wondering why I'm here." Before he could say anything else, she explained, "You mentioned needing some help here preparing for the calves. I don't know anyone looking for a job, but I thought I might be able to help out."

Jonas's eyebrows shot up in surprise. Her help out? The mere idea of it was laughable. Looking her over from head to toe, Jonas tried to take her in. Abigail was a very petite girl without the appearance of a muscle in her body. It was hard to picture her being able to lift a hammer—let alone knowing how to use one.

"I've helped my *daed*," Abigail explained as if she could read his uncertainty. Nodding, she went on to say, "Back when we moved to our homestead, I helped to build the house."

Helped to build the house? For all Jonas knew, that meant that her father had simply let her hand him nails.

Trying not to laugh in her face, Jonas forced himself to simply smile as he said, "Well, I appreciate it, but I wouldn't feel right letting a *maedel* work like that."

"*Ach*, I enjoy the work," Abigail tried to assure him.

Jonas deliberated carefully. On the one hand, he felt a deep sense of guilt at the idea of sending her back home when she had traveled all this way to help him. But on the other hand, the idea of having a young woman there on the farm working alongside him almost nauseated him. Finally, he determined that he would let her hand him things for a few hours to make her feel like she was being helpful, then send her home to her mother.

Flashing a smile, Jonas simply said, "All right. I guess I could use someone here to help me out. At least you can keep me company."

Abigail's grin reached full capacity as she assured Jonas, "I don't think you'll regret it."

That was the problem. Jonas already regretted it!

"Looks like your post there has the entire pen off kilter," Abigail announced as she joined him and pointed toward the left side of the calf pen. Cocking her head to one side, she scrutinized it carefully before saying, "I think if you bring that up just a couple inches, it will probably solve your entire problem."

Before Jonas could even ask what she was talking about, Abigail hurried to the other side of the pen and began implementing adjustments. Pointing at nails and screws, she tried to explain exactly how he could adjust the assembly to better suit his plans.

Somewhat in awe, Jonas stood back and watched Abigail work her magic on his pen. When she started calling for specific tools that she needed, he hurried to gather them for her and pass them her way.

Finishing the leveling of the pen, Abigail stood tall and inspected her handiwork. Cocking her head this way and then that, she gave it all a once-over before wiping her hands together and declaring, "I think that should do the trick. What do you think?"

Abigail turned to look at Jonas, who had to quickly shut his mouth. Shrugging, he laughed nervously and said, "I never would have guessed that you were that skilled." Giving her a sideways look, he asked, "How do you know so much about constructing things?"

His words seemed to please Abigail, and Jonas noticed a slight blush on her cheeks as she said, "I tried to tell you that I had built a house before. I've always liked working with wood and making things."

Letting out a whistle, Jonas admitted, "Well, I guess you sure surprised me. I thought that you had probably just helped out a little bit when your *daed* was building the house. I didn't expect that you actually knew so much." Finding himself a little nervous and even intimidated by her skills, he added, "I might be able to use your help more than I thought."

Abigail practically beamed, and she nodded as she said, "*Ya.* I was hoping you would feel that way. I can do almost anything...as long as it doesn't require a lot of strength and muscle."

Patting his arm, Jonas said, "Well, I guess the muscle is where I *kumm* in."

As soon as the words left his mouth, Jonas felt like he might die of embarrassment. What had gotten into him? He was never the type of person to try to impress young women with his brawn and strength. He immediately felt like smacking his head right into one of the large beams holding up the barn to knock some sense into himself.

Seeming not to notice his comment, Abigail was already pointing out changes that should be made to the next pen. She was an enigma, and Jonas wasn't quite sure what to make of her—or the feelings that she was causing to well up inside of him. A part of him felt intimidated by her—as if she was an unexpected source of competition— while another part of him was mesmerized. There was something captivating and magnetic about her that compelled Jonas to want to simply sit and study her.

Regardless of his conflicted feelings, Jonas was starting to see just how much Abigail might be able to help him with his project, and the idea of working with her seemed more appealing than it had before.

∞ ∞ ∞

Although she was focused on nailing a board in place, Abigail was well aware of the fact that Jonas's eyes hadn't left her from the moment that she arrived at his farm. Even when he handed her tools as she required them, his gaze never strayed from her. *He's in awe!* The knowledge made her heart swell.

From the moment that she first laid eyes on him, Abigail had known that there was something different about Jonas Smoker. He had managed to capture her heart and attention at a time when it seemed that no young man would ever be attractive to her, and Abigail was determined to capture his heart as well.

"So, Jonas Smoker," she said as she secured a new board in place, "tell me about your plans for this farm. When I pulled up in my buggy, I looked around, and it sure seems like you've got more than just raising calves in mind."

Jonas nodded and began to apprise her about his work and plans to try to expand the farm and how it was all coming along. Jonas chattered without reserve as they worked side by side to slowly transform the barn into a future home for calves.

His passion in relaying his plans for the future painted an absorbing picture, and Abigail could envision everything that he was saying. He was a young man with more than just an idea or far-out thought—he had definite, tangible goals and a plan to make them happen.

As they finished the fifth calf pen, Jonas straightened and stretched, reaching his arms above his head to ease his tired muscles, and suggested, "It's getting late. How about we go outside, and I'll show you around the farm before you have to leave?"

Abigail nodded, and a sweet smile spread across her face. She might not know much about farming, but she wanted to spend as much time with Jonas as possible, and she wanted to get to know as much about his life as she could.

Tipping the leftover nails back into their container, Abigail, too, rose, stretched, and followed Jonas outside toward the back of the house. Walking in step with him, she listened with interest as he shared his ideas of expanding the farm and new ways that the land could be used to earn money.

They stopped right in the midst of a large hay field, and Abigail reflexively closed her eyes and sucked in the fresh scent of grass and wildflowers. Smiling softly, she whispered, "I think I understand why you love this farm so much."

"*Ya*," Jonas agreed with a nod. "A lot of people can't see why the land is so important to me...but how could it not be? This is what *Gott* has made and has given to my *familye* to protect and use. I can't help but feel like it's one of the greatest gifts I have received."

Turning to look at Jonas, Abigail watched as his eyes roamed over the land. He looked like he was seeing it and soaking it all in for the first time. Abigail felt something deeper than simple attraction for him stirring within her.

Jonas Smoker was unlike anyone else in the community, and Abigail felt a kinship with him. He was someone who had a depth of character she had experienced in no other.

Closing her eyes once again, she tried to capture the entire scene in her mind. Standing there next to Jonas, she realized that this moment was what she wanted to experience for the rest of her time on earth. She wanted to be with Jonas Smoker, no matter what.

"Please, *Gott*," she breathed silently into the wind, "let it be so."

Abigail could only hope and pray that her good carpentry skills would be what it took for her to be able to gain Jonas's friendship and eventually win his heart.

Chapter Five

Abigail worked to try and finish up the last of the breakfast dishes as quickly as possible.

"I don't think that dish rag could go any faster if it had a fancy *Englisch* engine on it!" Colette commented as she stepped up beside her daughter, a tired smile on her thin face. "What are you in such a hurry to go do?"

Shrugging, Abigail tried to look less obvious in her rushing as she said, "Nothing too important, I suppose. I just want to get done quickly." Sucking in a deep breath, she added, "Jonas and I were planning to do a few more of the calf pens this morning."

Glancing at her mother out of the corner of her eye, Abigail observed a knowing look cross Colette's face. Colette grabbed a dish towel and began to dry the dishes as she said, "Seems like you have helped him plenty already. You have been out there the last two days.”

Abigail’s face started to grow warm. Knowing that her mother was keeping track made her somewhat uncomfortable.

Reaching out a hand and placing it gently on her daughter’s shoulder, Colette turned her so that she could look her in the eye as she said, “You know, Abigail, I don’t fault you one bit for trying to spend time with Jonas Smoker. I just hope that you’re not investing yourself in him for no *gut* reason.”

Running the dish cloth against one of the mugs, Abigail tried to keep her disappointment in check. She had wondered the same thing at least a dozen times that week. While she was becoming more smitten with Jonas by the day, she was starting to wonder if he actually saw her as anything more than simply a helping hand. Perhaps her mother was right and he was just a confirmed bachelor who had no interest in women.

As if reading Abigail’s mind, Colette used her thumb to lift her daughter’s chin and look her in the eye. Smiling at her, she said, “Don’t let me discourage you, *Liewi*. It’s better to try than to always wonder what might have been." Nodding her head toward the dishwater, she added, "I'll finish up with the dishes. You go on."

Abigail was so excited and anxious to go that she felt like clapping her hands together. Leaning over to give her mother a kiss on the cheek, she smiled brightly. "*Danki, Maem.* I appreciate it so much!"

Hurrying toward the door, Abigail stopped short when Colette called out to suggest, "Abigail, why don't you invite Jonas to *kumm* over for supper tonight? After all, he might enjoy the chance to see the house you helped to build—and see you when you're not covered in sawdust and sweat."

Invite him over for supper? The idea was so appealing, yet Abigail wondered if he would even agree. Nodding, she said, "I'll see if he will *kumm. Danki* again, *Maem.*"

Hurrying out the door, Abigail tied the strings of her prayer *kapp* so that it wouldn't blow off in the breeze and went to hitch up the buggy. At least getting Jonas to her mother's house might be a step in the right direction. Perhaps a little time together outside of the context of his farm would help him to stop viewing her as just a worker and more of a friend—or even something more. Abigail was well aware of the fact that her mother's biggest wish in life was to see her married; now that Jonas Smoker was a part of her life, she was beginning to think that it might be her goal as well.

∞ ∞ ∞

Abigail's heart mimicked the motion as her buggy jolted to a stop in front of the Smoker homestead. Instead of the growing familiarity with Jonas making visiting him feel easy, each time she pulled into Jonas's driveway, she found herself a little more nervous than the time before.

Abigail glanced around as she secured her horse to the hitching post adjacent to the barn, looking for any sign of Jonas. Disappointment dampened her anxious anticipation when he was nowhere in sight.

The sound of humming drifted on the warm breeze from inside the house out into the barnyard, and Abigail decided to make her way over to ask about Jonas. It was unusual for him not to be out in the barn or at least in the fields working.

Stepping up onto the white porch, Abigail took in a deep breath. Despite having been at Jonas's home the last two days, she had yet to even see his mother. Eagerness and dread alike at the possibility of meeting the woman filled Abigail. She could still recall her father's words about mothers-in-law—they alone hold the power to either make or break a relationship. If a young man's mother doesn't like you, you don't stand a chance in the world. Abigail had seen this reality play out in the lives of her elder brothers, and she wondered how Jonas's mother would perceive her and whether or not she would meet his mother's approval.

Raising her fist as she breathed a silent prayer for help, Abigail knocked on the door and stepped back to wait. The humming stopped, and footsteps sounded on the hardwood floor as the person approached.

The door swung open and revealed a middle-aged woman with salt-and-pepper hair pulled back beneath her prayer *kapp*. She looked tired and somewhat weary from life, yet her eyes seemed to light up when she caught sight of Abigail.

"*Gude daag!*" she said with a smile. "Can I help

you?"

Twisting her hands nervously together in front of her, Abigail smiled and said, "*Ya*. I'm looking for Jonas. Do you happen to know where he might be? I haven't seen him around the barnyard."

Nodding, the older woman clasped her dishrag between her hands as she explained, "He had to run into town to get some sort of seed for the back field." Laughing, she added, "That *bu* is always doing something else to expand the farm. Every time I think that he's done with it, he conjures up a new plan!" Motioning toward the house, she said, "Why don't you *kumm* in and wait for him?"

Abigail felt a wave of relief wash over her as Jonas's mother held out a hand and said, "I'm Barbara Smoker."

Taking her hand in a shake, Abigail felt hopeful that things were moving in the right direction. Smiling back at her, she said, "I'm Abigail Speicher."

Barbara's eyes narrowed and she asked, "Is your mother Colette Speicher?"

Giving another nod, Abigail said, "*Ya*, that would be her."

A look of surprise crossed Barbara's tired face

as she muttered, "Then your *daed* would be the one who died in the fire..."

Abigail suddenly felt a bit uncomfortable at the mention of her father's death, but to her relief, Barbara added, "*Ach.* Jonas lost his *daed*, too. I don't know if he's told you that or not."

Nodding, Abigail followed Jonas's mother to the chair that she offered at the kitchen table and watched as the older woman sliced them each a big piece of pound cake. Presenting the cake to her guest, Barbara continued to talk as she said, "Jonas was just a young man when his *daed* passed away. He was getting ready to start on his *Rumspringa*—but it was all cut short when his father passed. Instead, Jonas started focusing on tending to the farm. He has become a sort of recluse of sorts...and at such a young age."

Taking a bite of her cake, Abigail soaked in every word that the other woman spoke. She listened intently, her eyes narrowed as she focused. She was finally getting an inside view of the man she was pursuing.

"Jonas had to grow up at a young age," Barbara finally finished. Meeting Abigail's gaze once again, she stated, "He needs someone who understands him...but he's pushed everyone away. He's never let a *maedel* into his life until now. Until you." Reaching across the table to take Abigail's hand in her own, Barbara's eyes glistened as she spoke. "I think you might be the *maedel* that I've been praying for. Maybe you are the one who can help to heal Jonas's heart."

The words were heartfelt, yet it seemed like Mrs. Smoker was presenting Abigail with an overwhelming task. Shockingly enough, Abigail didn't find it to be too presumptuous. Instead, new unnamed emotions stirred within her. Perhaps the attraction that she felt toward Jonas was actually more than just romantic interest. Maybe the Lord truly had listened to Barbara's prayers and was using Abigail to answer them.

Squeezing the older woman's hand tenderly, Abigail smiled and whispered conspiratorially, "I hope I am."

The sound of an approaching buggy made them both sit up straighter in their chairs like two naughty children caught in a mischievous act. It wouldn't do to have Jonas catch his mother and hopefully future wife colluding about their relationship!

∞ ∞ ∞

The sight of Abigail's familiar buggy tied near the barn set off a surge of emotions through Jonas. Sometimes, he wasn't sure exactly what to think of the strange but beautiful girl who had managed to burst into his life in such an unconventional way.

While Jonas appreciated the work that she did and the help that she was lending to the calf project, he didn't particularly like the uncomfortable emotions that she stirred up and sent surging through his entire being. Abigail could make him feel so many strange things all at once that he wasn't sure where to even start in dealing with them.

Jonas saw her step out onto the porch as he glanced toward the house, and his heart somersaulted in his chest. She was truly a beautiful girl—perfect in almost every way. Sometimes, when he watched her working out in the barn, Jonas got so completely consumed with watching her that he felt like he lost all sense of time and sense in general. He often worried about what he might have said to her.

Lifting his hand to wave to her, Jonas called out, "I didn't know if you were planning to *kumm* today or not."

Smiling softly, Abigail assured him, "I said that I would, didn't I? I always try to keep my promises." She practically skipped over to his side. "What are we working on today?"

Within a few minutes, the two of them were busy in the barn, working side by side. Abigail had a drive to her that was unmatched by any other Jonas had ever seen. She was goal-oriented and determined to see a project through to the end; she made the ideal partner.

Laughing in amazement as Abigail finished up on another pen, Jonas said, "I don't think I've ever met anyone who can match you as a *gut* worker."

Turning her head to smile at him, Abigail explained, "I think I get it from my *daed*. He was always one to push for excellence." Her expression darkened as she added, "I miss him...a lot. Sometimes it feels like he's still with me when I'm doing things like working with wood and building things."

Jonas smiled softly and nodded in understanding. "I feel like my *daed's* with me when I'm able to bring to life his dreams of improving the farm."

There was something pleasant between them —a sort of camaraderie that Jonas had not shared with anyone else in the past. Abigail understood him in a way that few others in the community ever could. That knowledge made him simultaneously uncomfortable and happy.

"How would you like to see the house that he and I built together?" Abigail asked brazenly. "*Kumm* to supper with me and my *maem*... tonight."

The suggestion came as a curveball for Jonas. Shifting his weight from one foot to the other, he stammered knowing he looked like an idiot, "I...well...supper...that's...I don't know what my *maem* has planned..." Looking up into Abigail's expectant gaze, he finally admitted, "Well, I don't see how it could hurt. I'll be there."

The look of pure joy on her face spoke louder than words alone ever could, and Jonas was soon smiling right along with her. Her delight was contagious. There was something terribly exciting about the possibility of an evening spent at the home of the pretty Amish girl. But he determined that he wouldn't let his heart and his emotions get away from him. He was going to have to work hard to keep himself from allowing this to become a habit! He certainly didn't have room in his life for any women, and Abigail was starting to get dangerously close to being more important to him than he dared to admit.

Chapter Six

Jonas attempted to straighten a few pieces of unruly hair on the top of his head as he scrutinized his appearance in his bedroom mirror. His nerves were one giant convoluted mass. Biting down on his lower lip, he momentarily considered just skipping the meal entirely. Perhaps he could just send word to Abigail that he wasn't going to make it and hide away at home instead. No sooner had the idea crossed his mind when guilt swooped in to swallow it, like a hungry bird swooping in for an insect. He couldn't do that to Abigail after she and her mother had taken the time to prepare a meal for him. After all, she had done so much to help him out at the farm—he at least could be polite enough to go visit her and eat supper with her family.

Jonas made his way down the hall and then the

flight of stairs. His mother was sitting in a rocking chair by the empty fireplace, a book spread open on her lap. Jonas hadn't mentioned the meal invite to her yet. He dreaded the teasing that would no doubt follow.

Clearing his throat, Jonas took in a deep breath of air and asked, "*Maem*, you didn't have any big plans for supper, did you?"

Pinning a finger to mark her place and raising her gaze, Barbara looked over the top of her glasses and said, "*Nee*, just leftovers. Why?"

Swallowing hard, he admitted, "Abigail Speicher invited me to go to her place for supper so I could see the house that she helped to build with her *daed*. I figured it might be a *gut* idea. Since she's doing so much around here, it only seems right to see her craftsmanship firsthand." Even as the words left Jonas's mouth, he realized how ridiculous they sounded. He could feel his face turning red.

Barbara's expression instantly morphed to one of pure hope, which only added to Jonas's embarrassment. His face was growing so warm that were it possible, it would've burst into flames; he began fiddling with his shirt collar. Thankfully, his mother kept her mouth shut where teasing was concerned and only nodded her head. "*Ya.* That won't be a problem. I hope you have a *gut* time."

Mrs. Smoker looked back down at her book, yet Jonas could see her chewing on her lower lip, likely trying to hold in the words that were threatening to escape. Forcing himself to take in a deep breath, he turned and started out the door into the growing evening. It was time for him to make the journey back to the Speicher house.

Stepping back into the house for a moment, he raised his finger in his mother's direction and declared, "Don't get any ideas, *Maem!*" Then he bounded out the door and toward his waiting buggy.

Making her way to the window to peer out nervously, Abigail's heart raced in her chest. She could only hope that her mother wouldn't notice just how nervous she was. It was almost five o'clock, and she had told Jonas that supper would be served by quarter after. Surely, he would be arriving at any time now—unless he had decided not to show up. The thought taunted Abigail and made her doubt herself. She had come to care for Jonas more quickly than she thought possible, and the idea that he might simply not show up made her nerves get nervous!

"You know, if that *bu* doesn't *kumm* tonight, I don't think you should help him anymore," her mother opined from behind her. While Abigail knew that Colette's words were intended as words of wisdom, they only felt like salt on an open wound. She knew that what her mother was saying was true—if Jonas decided not to come to eat with them, it would be difficult for her to ever find a reason to spend time with him again. His choice that night would either open the door to a potential relationship or shut it firmly in her face.

The sight of an approaching buggy turned Abigail's anxiety into a relieved smile. Turning to her mother, she announced, "He's coming right now." Her mouth ached, such was the size of her unstoppable grin.

Hurrying to the front door, Abigail swung it open before Jonas could even bring the buggy to a stop. Making her way across the lawn, she didn't even care about the grass tickling her bare feet. Her mind was only focused on seeing Jonas and spending time with him.

"I was starting to worry that you wouldn't show up!" Abigail admitted as she made her way to Jonas's side.

He stepped down from the buggy and smiled. Somehow, he seemed slightly less at ease than usual. It almost felt like he recognized the weightiness of this meal together and the potential change it might signal in their relationship.

"Why wouldn't I show up?" he asked with a shrug, obviously trying to act nonchalant as he tied up his horse. "After all, we've gotten to be *gut* friends, and you've helped me a lot. Of course I'd want to meet your *maem* and get to see the home you helped to build."

At the description of being "friends," Abigail's joy deflated like a fully blown balloon released without being tied. Forcing herself to stand up straighter, she brushed the dark feeling away and determined to be a cheerful host. Directing Jonas toward the house, she explained, "Let's start by looking at the house from the outside. Supper's not quite out of the oven yet."

The sound of another buggy approaching took Abigail by total surprise. Turning around, her heart sank with a sickening thud when she recognized the familiar horse pulling none other than Pete Zook into the driveway.

Forcing herself to look directly at the man that she had scorned as a suitor, Abigail said, "Evening, Pete. Can I help you?"

Pulling his buggy to a stop, Pete gawped at her before turning his gaze to Jonas and then back to her. An expression that Abigail had never seen crossed his features. He appeared to be having a hard time swallowing before he finally stated, "Well, I was needing to get some supplies from the shop..."

"We're closed for the night," Abigail informed him curtly. Of course, she knew that wasn't Pete's reason for traveling out their way. He had most likely decided to come by simply to see if she was more open to his advances after his conversation with Colette. Crossing her arms against her chest, she declared, "You will have to *kumm* back another day."

Not even waiting for Pete to reply, she reached out and grabbed hold of Jonas's arm. Directing him toward the house, she said, "Let's start around back."

Abigail's heart lodged in her throat as she

listened for Pete's buggy to pull out of the driveway. Her bravado had been mainly on the outside! At her side, Jonas was chuckling as he asked, "A friend of yours?"

Shaking her head furiously, Abigail assured him, "Most definitely not. Yours?"

Now it was Jonas's turn to shake his head as he replied, "*Nee.* Afraid not. Pete Zook and I went to school together as *kinner*, and we got off on the wrong foot right from the start. He's no friend of mine. I think he'd consider himself more of an enemy."

Abigail chose to keep her mouth shut, but secretly, she thought that Pete might count her an enemy as well. She didn't like the way that he had looked at her and Jonas, and she had the troubling sense that he was going to stir up some kind of trouble.

Let him dare try and do something to destroy what I'm building with Jonas Smoker!

Walking past the flowers that surrounded the house, Abigail began to point out certain areas of the building's structure and how she had helped her father in the creation of the establishment. As they talked and laughed together, all thoughts of Pete Zook were relegated to the recesses of her mind. It all seemed so surreal to Abigail.

I'm actually having a young man over for supper! Not just any young man but the one-in-a-million young man who has stolen my heart.

Turning to look at Jonas, she pointed toward the roof and said, "*Daed* actually had me up there on the roof helping him to nail down shingles. It nearly scared my *maem* to death!"

Jonas laughed and said, "I would imagine so!" Looking up to the roof, he shielded his eyes from the still sharp evening sun. As he did so, the toe of his black boot caught on a rock, and he began to lunge forward. With no control or stability, he reached out and grabbed Abigail for support as he struggled to steady himself.

As she helped him regain his footing, Abigail felt herself almost magnetized to him. She stared into his face as she chuckled and said, "*Ach*, I should have pointed out that big rock!"

Standing up straighter, Jonas continued to hold onto her arm as he laughed along with her and said, "I think I need to pay more attention to where I'm going. *Ach*, I'm as goofy and unsteady as an old man."

Suddenly, Jonas stopped talking and simply stared at Abigail. The space between them, a mere few inches, crackled, and Abigail felt a tingle of excitement shimmy all the way up her neck and cause her to break out into goose bumps. *I wonder if he feels it, too?*

Suddenly feeling overwhelmingly awkward, Abigail became desperate to get away from him and steer his intense gaze elsewhere.

Jonas leaned forward as though he was going to press his lips against hers. It was what Abigail wanted with all her heart yet at the same time more unnerving than she could have ever imagined.

Almost involuntarily, she pivoted and pointed back toward the roof. "Like I was saying, right there is where my *daed* had me working."

Abigail prattled on with her story, and the magical moment fizzled to nothing. As soon as she interrupted it, she wished that she could turn back the hands of time and relive it. With every second that passed, she kicked herself for chickening out of their near kiss. However, she realized it had felt like too much too soon. *I hope that there will be other opportunities in the very near future!*

Jonas gave one last wave in Abigail's direction as he pulled his buggy away from the Speicher house. She'd said she needed to tend to the store the next morning, so she might not be able to help with the calf pens until the afternoon the following day.

Jonas was disappointed that he wouldn't see her for a whole morning—more disappointed than he wanted to admit, even to himself. Yet he realized that it was probably for the best. After the evening spent with Abigail and her mother, his eyes had been opened in an unexpected way.

"You're on the verge of losing it, *bu*," Jonas whispered to himself. Shaking his head, he reached up to rub his forehead. *What is happening to me? I've always been so level-headed where women are concerned!*

He had never been one to get lost in emotion or romance. He had been focused on the farm and nothing else, laughing at the mere suggestion that anything else might entice his attention.

But now...well, now Jonas wasn't sure where he stood at all.

When he had practically fallen into Abigail and grabbed onto her for support, Jonas looked into her eyes and saw something in those beautiful brown eyes—he saw his future. He had wanted to step forward and kiss her, grabbing her up and taking her in his arms. If she hadn't been the one to pull away and continue their conversation, he wasn't sure that he wouldn't have given in to his strange urge.

Jonas had enjoyed his evening with Abigail, but it was becoming obvious that he enjoyed it too much. Abigail Speicher was starting to feel like more than just a friend to him, and Jonas wasn't about to let that happen.

"You have to get away from her," he told himself. He was going to have to do whatever it took to protect himself and his goal to remain a confirmed bachelor forever.

Sitting up straighter in his seat, his mind raced as he considered the situation. Finally, he came up with a plan. The next morning, he would see about getting a few friends together to help him finish up the construction of the calf pens. Once they were finished, he could thank Abigail but assure her that her services were no longer needed. Yes, that was just what he was going to do. It might not be what he wanted to do, but Jonas was going to have to take some action to nip this relationship in the bud before it developed into something more serious.

Chapter Seven

Pete Zook had spent the better part of his night tossing and turning restlessly in bed, unable to get a wink of sleep. Images of Abigail had played through his mind nonstop—along with the horrible memory of seeing her in her back yard with none other than Jonas Smoker.

"Jonas Smoker," Pete muttered as he shook his head. He was practically seething with frustration and irritation. *How did Jonas Smoker manage to steal Abigail's attention?*

Abigail was one of the prettiest girls in the community, and even more importantly, she was one of the only girls who hadn't already found a suitor. Pete had determined that she would be the perfect match for him—until she rudely excused herself from their first and only buggy ride and escaped with her cousin.

"Jonas Smoker." Pete spoke his rival's name again. He had always felt like he and Jonas were in competition for everything at school; now it appeared that they were still in competition with one another in the field of courtship. The thought of Jonas getting something that Pete couldn't have, grated Pete intensely. *How dare Jonas, anyway? Everyone knows that Jonas has no interest at all in young women and has turned down any attempts at anyone finding him a match.*

He was supposedly married to his farm. So what was going on between him and Abigail?

Starting down the road, Pete headed in the direction of the only place he knew to turn. He was going to Abron Kauffman's house. If there was anybody whom he could trust, it would be his father's best friend—the bishop. Since Abron's only daughter had gotten married, Pete knew that the man was often home and more than happy to receive a guest.

Marching on up the road, his breathing quickened when he saw Abron's farmhouse come into view. Abron was sitting on the front porch with a book spread open on his lap. Throwing up a hand by manner of greeting, Pete called out, "Bishop!"

Looking up from his reading, the middle-aged man smiled and waved back. Setting his book aside, he pulled himself to his feet and said, "*Gude daag*, Pete Zook. How is your *daed* doing? Seems like I never get to sit down and chat with him anymore."

Shrugging, Pete hurried to say, "*Ach, Daed* is well. He mentioned just the other night wanting to stop by and see you sometime. I'm sure he'll make his way over here soon." Stepping up on the porch next to the bishop, Pete grew solemn as he said, "Bishop Kaufmann, I've got a dilemma…and I need your advice."

Pointing toward an empty rocking chair, Abron said, "Sit down, *Soh*, and let me know what's troubling you. I'm sure that together we can work out a solution."

Taking the offered seat, Pete appreciated the bishop's sincerity. With the help of the church leader, Pete was certain he would have no trouble solving this situation with Abigail and her new friend, Jonas Smoker.

Abigail glanced toward the clock that hung on the wall as she waited impatiently in the farm supply store. The hours were dragging by ever so slowly, and with each one's passing, she missed Jonas even more.

"*Kumm* on, *Maem*," she muttered to herself. Colette had an appointment at the chiropractor's office that morning, and she left Abigail to tend to the shop with the promise that she would be back soon to take over. Abigail was beginning to wonder if her mother had forgotten about her! It felt as though each minute was an hour!

Memories of the previous evening and her meal with Jonas brought a smile to Abigail's lips. They had certainly enjoyed a good time together, and Colette completely approved of Abigail's new friend.

"And *Maem* thought that he might like me," Abigail whispered excitedly into the silence of the empty warehouse. Her mother had assured her that while Jonas might be a confirmed bachelor, Colette had caught him casting glances in Abigail's direction that were far from uncaring. In fact, Colette was convinced that Jonas was already smitten.

"She said he will soon be in love." Abigail

recalled her mother's exact words and swooned at the mere memory.

Glancing out the window, her mind shifted back to thoughts of Pete Zook. She had been worried that the horrific man might return that day, but so far, there was no sign of him. If her mother could just return soon, then maybe Abigail could escape before he had a chance to appear.

While Abigail's future had looked very dismal only a few days ago, now it was starting to seem like the Lord might have something good in store for her. The possibility of a future with Jonas was tremendously exciting, and she was giddy about the possibility of what might be waiting just around the corner.

Nibbling her lip, Abigail leaned her weight against the top of the counter and smiled as she closed her eyes. Images of Jonas filled her mind, and she could hardly wait to be back at his farm working side by side.

***

Stepping back to view his friends' handiwork on the calf pens, Jonas shook his head in frustration. "*Ach*, you two!" he exclaimed as he pointed toward the pen that his friends had just completed. "How can that look *gut* to you?"

Standing up straighter and putting a hand against his back, Thomas Yoder's face bore a frown as he observed his newest project. "It looks fine to me!"

"*Ya*," Samuel Christner threw in with an emphatic nod. "It seems like it should hold a calf. This is exactly how my *daed* and I built ours on our farm!"

Stepping up closer to the pen, Jonas grabbed a hold of it and shook the gate, pointing to where the boards were shaking. "Look at that—do you actually call yourselves carpenters?"

Reaching out to give Jonas a playful pat on the shoulder, Thomas cheerfully reminded him, "Actually, we just call ourselves friends...friends who are helping you out without expecting anything in return."

Standing in solidarity, Samuel commented, "You're being pretty demanding for a guy who is asking for free labor!"

Jonas couldn't help but chuckle along with them. He hung his head and admitted, "I guess that's true. Sorry, fellows." It was just hard to get used to poor craftsmanship after he was used to experiencing so much more from Abigail.

Abigail. That girl kept finding her way into his mind again and again. Jonas wasn't sure why he couldn't just push her out of his thoughts for good. He had called his friends over to help with the building of the pens so that he would no longer need her help—or find himself tempted by the future that she offered.

"The main thing is that we just need to get finished as quickly as possible," Jonas declared. Even if he had to depend on pens that would only last through one round of calves, at least he could stay away from Abigail until his brain had settled back on his shoulders.

Watching his friends get back to work, Jonas couldn't help but automatically step forward to help them level up a board, just as he had watched Abigail do. At least he could still use the know-how that she provided during their time together. Surely, that much wouldn't be a risk!

"*Gude daag!*" A familiar female voice rang out from the doorway of the barn.

As soon as he heard the voice, Jonas's heart bucked and heaved like a cornered wild stallion in his chest. Bolting upright as though he had just heard a gun go off in his ear, he turned to the speaker. Sure enough, there stood Abigail in the doorway, a cheerful smile on her face.

"Abigail." He choked the name around a lump that was forming in his throat.

Oh my! Doesn't she look pretty this afternoon! Trying to regain his sense, he hurried over to her side after motioning for Thomas and Samuel to continue working.

"Jonas." Abigail smiled when he reached her side, "Sorry I took so long. *Maem's* appointment went longer than I expected."

Longer than she had expected and shorter than Jonas had hoped! Pointing toward the construction, he explained, "It's perfectly fine. I don't expect you to spend every hour of your life here working and helping me when you have other responsibilities. After all, you have your *Maem* to help and the store to tend to. Besides, some friends have *kumm* to help."

Jonas motioned toward Samuel and Thomas just in time for her to see Samuel hit his thumb with a hammer and let out a yelp of pain.

"Well, that should help to get the work done faster!" Abigail declared. If she was at all taken aback or disappointed, she didn't let her feelings show. Pushing past Jonas, she walked to the corner where the young men were working and began to survey their work. Jonas didn't have to see her face to know that she would be unhappy with the outcome.

"*Gude daag*, Abi!" Thomas called out cheerfully. "I didn't expect to see you until Sunday night at the *sing*!"

"What do you think of our work, Abi?" Samuel threw in his own question.

Jonas felt his hackles instantly go up. Why were his friends so well acquainted with Abigail? It almost seemed like they were intruding on his personal territory. *How dare they try to talk to* my *Abigail!*

While Jonas knew that his feelings were silly and unwarranted, he could do nothing to stop them. He found himself marching across the barn with a new purpose in his step, suddenly determined to take over and send Abigail packing. Just because he didn't want Abigail for himself didn't mean that he wanted one of his friends to have her instead!

"You all are doing a *gut* job," Abigail said kindly although Jonas could hear the hesitancy in her voice, "but I think that you'd have some better luck keeping the fence standing if you added a supportive beam right here."

Before Jonas could reach her side, Abigail had already forced her way into the newly constructed calf pen and was reaching for a board, asking Thomas to hold it up as she hammered it in place.

"Well, look at that!" Samuel exclaimed once she had put up the new piece. "Abi you truly know what you're doing."

Abigail's face began to grow pink at the compliment, and she looked down at the barn floor as she declared, "I never tried to keep it a secret that I am *gut* with carpentry."

"Hey, we need you here!" Thomas spoke up, his own face breaking out in a wide grin before he turned to look at Jonas. "We need Abigail to stay!" Making it doubly impossible for Jonas to refuse his request, he added, "If she leaves, then I'm going, too." Turning back to Abigail, he asked, "You will help, won't you?"

Practically beaming with mingled pride and happiness, Abigail replied, "That was my plan."

Jonas could hardly believe his ears. How had his best attempts at getting away from Abigail gone so horribly awry? Rather than providing an excuse to push her away, his friends had just been instrumental in convincing her to stay and help.

Shaking his head, Jonas had no clue what he should do next. Perhaps his best course of action was to simply try to keep his heart in place and his brain on straight until this project was finished and he could distance himself from Abigail Speicher for good!

∞ ∞ ∞

Standing inside his small house, Abron Kauffman mulled over the quandary that Pete Zook had just presented to him.

Pete had always been one of Abron's favorite young men in the community. Of course, it didn't hurt that Pete's father was one of Abron's closest childhood friends. The Zooks were a good family, and Abron was always determined to do whatever necessary to help them.

"And now they need help," Abron muttered to himself. Abron had always been a firm believer that courting couples needed to take relationships seriously. As Pete had explained, Abigail Speicher agreed to go out riding with him—that was as good as agreeing to be courted by him—only to have Pete discover her in the company of another young man a few days later.

"I won't tolerate that kind of behavior in my *gmay*," Abron voiced aloud as he reached for a teacup and poured himself some black tea. Sipping the bitter liquid, he shook his head and said, "*Nee*, things like that need to be nipped in the bud—no matter what it may take."

After his conversation with Pete, he was pretty sure the young man was up for the task and had plenty of ammunition to ensure that Jonas Smoker would be out of the picture for good! Now it was just up to Pete to take action and do what they had discussed.

Chapter Eight

Working with the boys all day had been different for Abigail. While she appreciated their help and even enjoyed the friendly banter that she shared with Thomas and Samuel, it had been hard not to be sad about the situation with Jonas.

He's pushing me away. Abigail would have been an idiot not to see what was so obvious.

Jonas had done everything in his power to keep a safe distance between the two of them all afternoon. When evening came, he swiftly agreed to give his other helpers a ride home in his buggy, leaving Abigail standing alone beside her own.

"I'm losing him," Abigail whispered under her breath, and tears prickled, then filled her eyes as she watched him drive away. A dark and hopeless cloud shrouded itself over her entire being. Why did it seem like the closer she got to Jonas, the harder he worked to get away from her? Perhaps they simply weren't meant to be. Maybe Jonas viewed her as just a nuisance and the attraction was only one-sided. How horrible that would be!

Standing up straighter, Abigail turned to her buggy and prepared for the long, lonely, painful ride back home.

"Do you have to leave just yet? I've got something for your *maem* in here!" The voice of Barbara Smoker stopped Abigail in her tracks, and she turned around in surprise. There on the front porch stood Jonas's mother, a dishrag in her hands and a smile on her face. As if Abigail hadn't understood her, she waved the dishrag in her direction and repeated, "*Kumm* in for a minute!"

Shrugging, Abigail turned and made her way to the Smoker house.

"Sorry for not having this ready sooner," Barbara said, "but I told Colette at the last quilting bee about my zucchini squash casserole, and she wanted to try some." Turning to the oven, she pulled out a casserole dish and set it on the table. "I baked one just for you all...and I'm sending the recipe along."

Abigail's heart swelled in her chest. How sweet Jonas's mother was. Cocking her head to one side, she looked at the delicious dish as she assured her, "*Ach*, that's so kind of you, but you didn't have to do so much for us!"

Waving the dishrag toward her, Barbara assured her, "It's what I wanted to do. Besides, you have done so much for me and Jonas—this is nothing in comparison." Pointing at the seat at the head of the table, she suggested, "How about you let that thing cool for a few minutes while we have some iced tea?"

The idea of the treat sounded wonderful. Abigail sat down and watched as Barbara fixed the drinks before sitting down next to her.

"I appreciate everything you've done for us... especially for Jonas," Barbara stated as she stirred some honey into her tea.

Feeling her throat thickening with emotion, Abigail tried to deflect her comment as she said, "*Ach*, it's nothing. I enjoy the work."

Studying Abigail seriously, Barbara returned, "It's meant the world to me and to Jonas." She laughed softly and added, "I have not seen my *soh* happier since his *daed* died. I think he feels at home with you. And I couldn't believe that he went to eat with your *familye* last night!"

Abigail couldn't withhold her comments any

longer. Shaking her head furiously, she exclaimed, "Well, he has a funny way of showing it. I care for your *soh*, Mrs. Smoker, but he's not an easy one to get close to. In fact, as soon as I started to feel like we were becoming friends, he pushed me away from him."

As soon as the words left her lips, Abigail recoiled. She had been too harsh, and she knew it. She instantly regretted telling Barbara so much.

To her astonishment, Jonas's mother appeared neither surprised nor upset. Instead, she just reached out to put a hand on top of Abigail's as she whispered, "You love him, don't you?"

Feeling her lower lip start to tremble, Abigail admitted what she had to no one else. "*Ya*. I'm starting to. I know we haven't known each other long, but he's the only one I've ever felt this way about."

Giving her hand a loving squeeze, Barbara looked imploringly at her as she said, "Then don't give up on him, Abigail. Ever since his *daed* passed away, he's built a wall around his heart that's been impenetrable. He won't let anyone get close to him."

"But why?" Abigail pressed, reaching up to openly wipe tears from her eyes.

Sighing deeply, his mother explained, "It all started when his *daed* passed away. I just think it happened so unexpectedly that Jonas decided that no one was safe, no one is invincible in this life—which is true. *Gott* can call us home at any time. But we can't shut our hearts off to everyone else just because there's a chance we might lose them." Tears shimmered in her own eyes as she whispered, "My married life was the happiest experience that I could have ever imagined. And I wouldn't give up those years for anything. I just worry Jonas is going to miss out on everything valuable in life if he keeps going down this path! He thinks this is his *Gott*-ordained path, but I can't believe that's really true. It's just his way of avoiding getting hurt."

Abigail's heart ached with compassion. She knew all too well what it was like to lose a parent and the pain that went along with it. Perhaps Jonas truly was trying to protect himself.

"My *soh* cares for you, Abigail Speicher," Barbara said bluntly without a hint of uncertainty in her voice, "but it's up to you whether you will let him turn you away or whether you'll fight for him until that love can finally blossom."

Abigail nodded wordlessly. It felt like an

impossible mission, but if the Lord was by her side, she knew that it could happen. Her determination, which had all but withered, was strengthened, and she sat up with a new resolve as she declared, "I'm not going to let him push me away."

Abigail was going to keep fighting to get into Jonas's heart, even if it took her last breath to get there!

∞ ∞ ∞

Jonas intentionally stayed away from home as long as possible, trying to give Abigail plenty of time to be on her way back to her own house. The day with her working alongside his friends had only done more to confuse him and addle his brain.

Samuel and Thomas had talked of nothing but Abigail the entire ride back to their homes. While Samuel already had a girlfriend, even he was willing to admit that she was one of the finest catches in the community. Thomas outright declared that she was beautiful, smart, and talented in every way.

Jonas had kept his mouth shut, but he secretly

agreed with every word that they said. How could he not? Abigail Speicher managed to be everything that an Amish man could want in a potential wife.

"If only I was the type to want a *fraa*," Jonas muttered to himself. Yet, even as he tried to remind himself why he didn't want a spouse, he envisioned what their lives might be like if they were actually married. He thought of them working together to make his goals for the farm a reality.

How could he be allowing himself to even entertain thoughts of her as a lifelong partner? Shaking his head, Jonas muttered to himself, "Jonas, you are an idiot!"

Pulling his buggy up to the Smoker home, he worked to unhitch the horse and then lead it into a pen in the barn. Stopping by the pens that Abigail had so lovingly built, he ran a hand across the top of one of them and sighed deeply into the growing dimness.

"You sure seem thoughtful tonight." His mother's voice startled him, and he chuckled when he looked up to see that she had managed to sneak into the barn unbeknownst to him.

As Barbara walked over to the calf pens, Jonas shrugged and said, "I guess I'm just tired. It's been a long, busy day."

Barbara seemed to be inspecting the craftsmanship on the pens before she announced, "You sure are doing a *gut* job with these."

Unable to take all the credit, Jonas pointed out, "Well, it's not just me working on them, that's for sure. I had the help of Thomas and Samuel…and Abigail." As soon as her name touched his lips, Jonas worried that he might choke. His emotions were in such turmoil he didn't know how to keep them in check.

"*Ya*," Barbara agreed with a nod. "You have some *gut* friends. I think I'm especially impressed with Abigail…she's *kumm* out here every afternoon to help you, and she hardly knows you at all. As far as I know, you've never done anything for her."

His mother's words pulled at Jonas's heart. It was true. Abigail had gone from being a stranger to someone who went well out of her way to help him. She had a heart of gold that was impossible to ignore.

Nodding slowly, Jonas said, "She is truly one of a kind."

Stepping closer to her son, Barbara patted him on the shoulder and said, "I know how you feel about trying to stay away from relationships, Jonas. But you'd be a foolish young man not to at least hang onto her as a friend."

Her words, though serious, were spoken with the soft kindness of a mother. Jonas knew how right she was. Without another word, Barbara turned and started toward the house, leaving Jonas all alone with his thoughts. He hated being left to be assailed by the myriad of mixed musings.

Shaking his head slowly, Jonas whispered, "What am I to do, *Gott*?"

He had been so sure that his life was on a set course, one that would ensure that he succeeded in making his father's dreams a reality. Now, he wasn't sure about anything. What if he had been wrong? What if the Lord had actually put Abigail in his life for a reason? What if she was truly supposed to be a part of Jonas's destiny? Wouldn't he be missing God's blessings if he turned down such a wonderful opportunity?

Jonas wished that he had the answers to all of life's dilemmas. For now, all he was going to do was focus on praying about it and trying to get some sleep. Perhaps he could get a better grasp on his future by allowing the chaos to settle and opening his heart to hear God's guidance.

Chapter Nine

Putting another bucket of nails in place, Abigail stepped back to observe her handiwork and rubbed her hands together. Glancing toward her mother, who was busy going over the books at the register, Abigail felt desperate to make her escape. Ever since her conversation with Barbara, she had been more determined than ever to ensure that she was able to break down the crusty barrier around Jonas's heart.

"Well, I'm all done stocking the shelves," Abigail said with a smile.

Looking up at her daughter, Colette let out a sigh and said, "I suppose I know where you want to go next." Although her tone was somewhat teasing, it was tinged with sadness.

Abigail knew that her mother was getting weary waiting to see her youngest daughter married. Colette was desperate to ensure that Abigail had a home and a life of her own before the Lord called Colette home. How Abigail wished that she could make that dream of her mother's a reality!

Almost as if she could read her daughter's thoughts, Colette reached across the space between them to cup Abigail's chin in her hands. Lowering her voice to a whisper, she said, "Remember, I told you that he does like you. Keep hanging in there. He will *kumm* around...I'm just praying that it's before *Gott* calls me to His side."

The words gave Abigail a sense of hope in her heart, and she leaned forward to throw an arm around her mother in a hug. How glad she was to have the support and the love of her mother as she waited on Jonas to finally realize what was right in front of him.

A knock on the shop door made both Speicher women jump in surprise. Abigail looked up in time to see none other than Jonas himself poke his head in through the open space, a smile on his lips.

"Knock, knock!" he called out playfully as he pushed the door open "Anybody home?"

Glancing at her mother, Abigail could see that Colette mirrored her own surprise.

"*Ya, kumm* on in!" Abigail returned once she regained her senses.

Stepping into the shop, Jonas announced, "I realized that we were all out of nails, and I wasn't sure if you would know to bring some by today." Pausing for a moment, he asked, "You *are* coming to help with the pens, aren't you?" Lowering his voice a little, he added, "I'm afraid we're hopeless without you. Samuel and Thomas are there again, but they don't do much other than make mistakes for you to fix."

Abigail laughed out loud, her heart suddenly feeling lighter than ever before. Trying to take the compliment in her stride, she said, "*Ach*, I think that they try their best!"

Nodding his head, Jonas returned, "That's the worst part of it. They *do* try their best, so there's no hope of them improving."

Shaking her head with another laugh, Abigail said, "I'll go pick those nails out for you."

Hurrying over to the area where she had just stacked the boxes of nails, she picked one up and brought it to the front of the store. Handing Colette some money, Jonas's eyes never seemed to leave Abigail as he asked, "Since I'm heading the same direction as you, is there any chance you'd take a ride with me?" Almost as if to make sure that she didn't misread his meaning, he hurried to add, "There aren't very many houses between here and there—I don't think anyone will see us and get the wrong idea."

Abigail didn't think it was possible for them to get the wrong idea—not if it became the right idea! She knew that her face was practically beaming as she nodded and said, "*Ya*, that would be great—if my *maem* is done with my help, that is."

Abigail glanced toward her mother, who was nodding her head furiously.

"Of course," insisted Colette. "You go on. You two have a *gut* time and get a lot of work done!"

Abigail couldn't remember a time since her father's death that she had seen such a happy twinkle in her mother's eye. Hopefully, it was the first of many more to come!

Driving his buggy down the road, Jonas could scarcely believe what he was doing. He had never taken a girl on a buggy ride, and he certainly hadn't planned to start now. Yet, it seemed that after sleeping on his mixed feelings about Abigail, he had actually woken with a twinge of interest in stepping out of his ordinary routine.

Turning to glance at her as he guided his buggy down the road, Jonas listened as she prattled on, telling a story about finding a snake in the garden the previous evening. While the story was interesting, it was hard for Jonas to keep his thoughts on the words coming off her lips. Instead, his mind was racing in so many different directions.

What if God truly had a plan for him and the beautiful young Amish girl?

For the first time in his life, Jonas actually hoped that things weren't going according to his plan. Perhaps it was time to throw caution to the wind and simply let his heart open up to this sweet girl that God had brought into his life. Perhaps it was time to stop trying to hide his heart away and let himself start to care for someone other than himself instead. The entire process seemed scary yet at the same time, strangely exciting.

Picking some green beans from the plant, Abigail smiled to herself as she dropped the fresh young veggies into her bucket. It was the cool of the day, making the garden work more pleasant. Colette was inside lying down, but Abigail didn't mind being alone. She was enjoying the chance to bask in her own thoughts and enjoy reminiscing about the day.

"It was a perfect day," she whispered under her breath. *Well, maybe not completely perfect but certainly close enough.*

Jonas made no declarations of love to her, and he hadn't attempted to try to say anything particularly romantic to her, but the fact that he offered her a ride to and from her home to his farm seemed monumental. His heart might still be hardened against the idea of marriage, but at least he was softening to being open to a sort of friendship. They had even enjoyed a pleasant conversation during the trip.

The sound of an approaching buggy ripped Abigail away from her thoughts. Hope that it was Jonas and fear that Pete might have returned warred within her, both causing anxiety. As she pulled herself into a standing position, she dusted off her skirt and started toward the front of the house. Rounding the corner of the house, she almost walked directly into Thomas Yoder.

Her eyes widened in surprise as she looked up at him and laughed, "*Ach*, I'm sorry! I didn't expect you to be standing here." Actually, she had no clue why Jonas's friend was there. Trying to wager a guess, she suggested, "Are you needing something from the store?"

Shaking his head, Thomas replied, "*Nee*, nothing like that. It's you that I've *kumm* to see, Abigail," with an odd look in his eye.

Instantly, her mind filled with frightening thoughts about what Thomas might be coming to say. *Perhaps he's made this visit in an attempt to try and convince me that I'm wasting my time on Jonas. Or, worse yet, maybe Jonas himself asked Thomas to tell me that he isn't interested in me.*

Clearing her throat, Abigail pointed toward a lawn table with chairs near the garden and suggested, "How about we go back there and sit?"

Nodding, Thomas followed her around back. But when she sat down, he remained standing in front of her, his black felt hat clasped in his hands.

Abigail's nerves were knotted, and she was growing more nervous by the minute. *What on earth could he be preparing to say?*

Shifting her weight in her seat, she cleared her throat to fill the awkward silence before finally asking, "What can I do for you, Thomas?"

Smiling a little sheepishly, Thomas looked down at the ground as he admitted, "You're a *gut* carpenter, Abigail. Truth be told, you're better than all of us working on Jonas's project."

The compliment was nice but did little to appease Abigail's uncertainty. She wondered if Jonas might have had Thomas come tell her not to return to the job site. That seemed very like Jonas—open his heart one minute and then slam it totally shut the next.

"I try my best," she finally murmured.

Nodding back at her, Thomas said, "We've been lucky to have you there...but it's more than just that. I feel like I've been lucky to get to spend time around you at all."

Abigail frowned as she tried to make sense of his ambiguous words and found herself growing even more nervous than before. *Could Thomas mean...*

"I respect you a lot, Abigail. I respect you, and I admire you." Looking up sheepishly, Thomas's face was as red as a beet as he searched out Abigail's gaze and confessed, "I... I like you, Abigail. I like you a lot. You're not like any other *maedel* that I've ever met. I was wondering if you would be...I mean...I guess I'm asking..."

Suddenly, the point of his visit became crystal clear. Thomas had come to ask her if she wanted to court. Watching him stumble over his words, Abigail felt instant sympathy for him. Sympathy *and* guilt. She hated the idea of breaking his heart, but what else could she do? She was going to have to be honest with him.

Pulling herself to her feet, Abigail interrupted him before he could go any further. Closing her eyes, she braced herself as she tried to decide exactly how she could turn him down in the most gentle of ways while preserving his dignity and their friendship. Opening her eyes slowly, she looked at Thomas and gave a soft shake of her head. "Thomas, you are a *gut* young *mann*. I enjoy your company, and you're a great friend. A few weeks ago, I would have gladly taken you up on your offer...but..." Her voice trailed off as she pondered just how much she should tell him.

Looking straight at him, she decided to be completely honest and tell the truth. "Thomas, my heart belongs to another already."

Thomas's face seemed to cloud over with

confusion that was then replaced with surprise. Lowering his voice, he asked, "You mean…Jonas?"

Now the one with a red face, Abigail nodded. "*Ya.*"

"But Jonas…Jonas doesn't even like *maed!*" Thomas protested with an incredulous shake of his head. "He's a confirmed old bachelor. You don't stand a chance with him. I can promise you that he'll never *kumm* to you and ask to court you. You'll be alone forever if you wait for him!"

The words were sharp and pierced Abigail's heart like a set of well-aimed daggers. The reality of his statement was so powerful that her knees practically buckled under their weight. Sucking in a deep breath, she shrugged and said, "If that's the truth, then I'll accept it. It's a gamble that I'm willing to make. I'm falling in love with Jonas Smoker…and Jonas is the only one who will ever have my heart."

Thomas looked disappointed but more shocked than anything else. Finally, he let out what sounded like a chuckle and declared, "Well, I guess that's the way things go. Jonas has got himself a *gut* catch…I just hope he's smart enough to recognize something *gut* when it's right in front of his face!" Growing serious, he asked, "Can we just forget this ever happened between us? And can we still be friends?”

Breathing a sigh of relief, Abigail gushed, “Of course! I’d love that, Thomas.” While she valued Thomas’s friendship, she would never have a place for him in her heart. That was reserved for Jonas alone.

Chapter Ten

bigail had just finished one of the last calf pens and was preparing for Jonas to take her home when Barbara came bustling out of the house, a happy smile lighting up her face.

Thomas and Samuel had already left for the day, and Abigail was anticipating a fun ride home with Jonas. While things between her and Thomas had initially been a bit awkward, they improved quickly and went back to normal. Thomas was now talking to another girl from a nearby community, and it seemed that his feelings of interest in Abigail were long gone.

While Abigail continued to work at Jonas's house on an almost daily basis, he had taken her to and from their houses every day. The time that they spent together was the most joyful that either could remember in recent years, with them laughing and sharing stories during the rides. Abigail treasured watching Jonas turn into someone who had truly become a dear friend. And maybe something more? She could only hope and pray that it was true that his feelings for her were beginning to grow into so much more from the foundation of friendship.

"You two, wait!" Barbara called out as she made her way to the buggy. "Before you run off, I wanted to ask you something, Abigail. I know that Jonas went to your house for supper the other night. Would you and your *maem* be willing to *kumm* over here tomorrow night? After all, it's only fair that I get to enjoy your company, too!"

Abigail glanced at Jonas and was happy to see that he was nodding his own approval.

Turning back to Barbara, Abigail smiled and said, "It would be a pleasure. I'll have to talk to my *maem*, but I'm sure that she'll be happy to *kumm* along!"

Giving a quick wave in their direction, Barbara announced, "Then it's settled! I'll look forward to having you both over tomorrow night." With that, she turned and started back into the house, leaving Abigail and Jonas alone.

Climbing up into the buggy seat, Abigail was floating on a cloud. She turned to look at Jonas as he sat down beside her. "You don't mind us coming for supper, do you?"

Shaking his head, Jonas smiled and said, "*Ach*, of course not! Nothing would make me happier." As he clicked his tongue for the horses to move forward, Jonas shifted uncomfortably in his seat. While conversation between the two of them generally came easily enough, this time, it felt a little strained.

Trying to fill in the void, Abigail spoke up. "I think I told you that I have to run a few errands in town tomorrow, so I won't be able to help much with the pens. If we're coming over for supper, would you be all right with me and *Maem* just waiting to *kumm* until evening? I hate to skip out on a day of work, but it would give me time to help her with the shopping."

Smiling softly, Jonas nodded again before admitting, "I don't know how much will actually get accomplished on the project without you, but that will be fine." His smile turning into a grin, he added, "Just be prepared that the next workday, you will probably have to start by fixing all our mistakes."

The two of them laughed along together, but silence quickly descended again. Abigail found herself wondering if she had done something to offend Jonas or make him feel bad. She shifted uncomfortably against the wooden seat, trying to come up with something else that she could say.

To her surprise, Jonas began to speak. "Abigail, I have appreciated everything that you've done to help me out," he stated, his voice full of sincerity. "Without you, my dreams for the farm wouldn't be nearly as far along."

Although his words seemed fairly noncommittal, his voice held a tenderness that Abigail hadn't heard before. She looked up and met his unexpectedly warm gaze as he added, "I didn't realize just how much I needed help until you came along. In fact, I hadn't realized how much I needed someone else in my life."

"It's been my pleasure to help—" Abigail started to assure him, but Jonas cut her short.

"Abigail, I've always been a loner, and it seems like that's just a part of who I am. But since I've gotten to know you...well, I've started wondering exactly what I think about being a bachelor forever. You have made me realize that there might be more to life than just going it alone."

The words felt like butterfly kisses landing on Abigail's cheeks. Her eyes filled with happy tears, and she had to work hard to keep her jaw from trembling.

"I don't want to make any bold promises right now," Jonas told her as he gripped the reins tighter in his hands, "because I'm not sure what my heart can handle. It's hard for me to let down my guard and try to love someone else. I guess it's because I've lost so much…"

Reaching out a hand, Abigail put it tenderly on his and leaned in to whisper, "It's okay. I understand. There's no rush at all."

Jonas turned his hand over and intertwining their fingers together, gave her hand a squeeze. Abigail meant her words: there truly was no rush. She loved Jonas, and that was never going to change. If it took ten years for them to actually start courting, that would be fine. All that she cared about was knowing that he was in her future.

As he watched Abigail walking to the front

door of the Speicher home, Jonas had to swallow his heart from up in his throat. She looked so beautiful as she disappeared into the farmhouse.

"And she may be mine," Jonas whispered to himself as he clicked his tongue and urged the horse to move the buggy forward.

The willingness to put his heart on the line had come as a sudden, spur-of-the-moment decision, but he made it with conviction. Each day, Jonas had grown closer and closer to Abigail, falling more in love with her by the minute. He had grown to appreciate her and knew that he wanted her in his life. Once he allowed himself to consider the possibility of being in a relationship with her, his initial twinge of desire had quickly developed into a full-blown desperate need.

"*Gott* has brought us together," Jonas assured himself as he guided the buggy forward. Abigail was one girl that he knew was worth putting his heart on the line for, and he trusted her implicitly. His entire future was starting to look very different from what he had ever imagined, and strangely enough, excitement was stirring in him.

How much more pleasant life might be if he could actually have a sweet girl like Abigail by his side. She had already done so much for Jonas and his mother. She had proven herself by going out of her way to make his dreams for the farm a reality, taking countless hours of her life and dedicating them to pure work for nothing other than gratitude. She was kind and gentle with people yet strong and hardworking. As much time as Jonas had spent around her, he never heard her speak a harsh word to anyone, and she could be humorous and lighthearted without a hint of gossip or slanderous talk. She surpassed every other woman that Jonas had ever known, and he couldn't help but think that when Proverbs 31 was penned, the author must surely have had a woman like Abigail in mind. If anybody would be the best life partner for him, it would be Abigail Speicher.

Clicking his tongue for the horse to move a little faster, Jonas's lips broadened into a smile. He could hardly wait for the meal that their families would share together the following evening. The way he felt in that moment, nothing could dampen his spirits!

Chapter Eleven

bigail shifted the weight of the package she carried as she walked down the road. She had enjoyed the morning of shopping with her mother in town, thanks to a paid driver. When Colette returned home and remembered that she had forgotten a bag of sugar, Abigail was happy to make the short walk down the road to the Amish-run general store.

While Abigail was tired from the long trip and the shopping experience, she had enjoyed the opportunity to go for a walk and spend some time alone with her thoughts. Life had so much excitement unfolding in it that she reveled in basking in the joy of imagining her future with Jonas. Closing her eyes, she breathed in the scent of fresh flowers and spring air.

Abigail turned her head at the sound of a buggy clip-clopping up behind her to see who might be approaching. As soon as she recognized the driver, her lighthearted mood fizzled out and her heart lurched with dread in her chest.

"Whoa there!" the driver called out to his horse, working to slow the buggy so that it came to a stop beside her.

Pete Zook.

Abigail didn't want to interact with him, and she was annoyed that he had stopped his buggy next to her. *What on earth could he want?* She had been hopeful that after seeing her with Jonas, he would have gotten the idea and stayed away.

"Abigail, I've been meaning to talk to you!" Pete called out as he stepped down from his buggy.

Deciding to at least be polite and give him her attention, Abigail stopped and turned to look at him. Steeling herself for whatever might be ahead, she said, "Pete, I'm afraid that there's nothing left for us to talk about. *Danki* for the buggy ride the other day, but I don't think we're meant to be a couple."

"Yes, I know," Pete assured with a shake of his head. His honesty was out of character! Stepping closer to her, he announced, "I don't think that we're a *gut* couple, either, but I needed you to know what's being said around the *gmay* about you."

Abigail raised her eyebrows. *About* me? *What on earth can they be saying? I've never done anything to bring about slander to my name! Surely, Pete is mistaken.* The idea of what gossip might do to her mother instantly filled her heart with dread.

"I went to see Bishop Kauffman the other night," Pete said as he looked down at the ground, his eyes growing serious. "He's my next-door *nochber*, you know. He was asking me about what was going on. Some people saw us riding together and assumed we were a courting couple. Then others saw you and Jonas together…" He shook his head sadly and said, "Well, it's now going around town that you're a bit of a run around. People think that you are allowing multiple young men to court you at the same time."

Abigail's heart skipped a few beats, and her limbs turned to jelly in shock. She gaped at Pete as a sinking feeling overtook her.

"*Ach*, Pete!" she exclaimed with a shake of her head. "It was nothing like that! You have to know it."

Nodding, Pete looked up to meet her eyes as he replied, "I know that, Abi! I never thought that you were that kind of *maedel*. We were never anything serious. I just hate it that others think that you are a rather loose *maedel*."

Abigail could hardly believe her ears. How could people be saying such things? Gossip like this might completely destroy her character and her reputation. What if her mother heard this at the quilting circle? Colette would be crushed. She put a lot of importance in their standing in the community. Even worse, what if Barbara heard it? Or Jonas himself? News like this would surely destroy all his new faith in her!

"Does Bishop Kauffman believe that?" Abigail asked incredulously.

Shrugging, Pete said, "*Ach*, I tried to explain it to him, but he said that he wanted to talk to you in person."

Grabbing her skirt with one hand, Abigail tried to calculate just how much of a detour it would be for her to go straight to the bishop's house and talk to him. "I've got to go talk to him and get this settled. He has to know the truth, and he has to set things right!"

Noticing her distress, Pete pointed toward his buggy and suggested, "How about you get in the buggy, and I'll take you. You can get there much faster that way!"

Never would Abigail have imagined accepting

Pete's offer of a ride, but in that moment, she hardly cared at all. She would ride with almost anyone if she had to, just so long as she could get the truth sorted out with the bishop. Nodding, she said, "*Danki, Danki* so much, Pete!"

Climbing up onto the buggy seat, Abigail's heart pounded wildly in her chest. If she had any hope at all of reclaiming her good name and stopping the gossip before it got out of control, she had to make things right immediately. Setting her grocery bag at her feet, she held on to the sides of the buggy for dear life. She hoped with everything in her that this mess could get settled before it was blown out of proportion and destroyed her future.

Whistling as he carried a pile of boards into the barn, Jonas looked over the work that his friends had just accomplished and smiled, "It's looking *gut, buwe*. Once Abigail gets here tonight, I'll have her look them over and see what she thinks of them. If we get the go-ahead, I'll confirm that we're finished with those pens."

"*Ya*, got to get Abi's approval on everything,"

Samuel teased.

"*Ach*, you know it!" Thomas quipped. "Abigail is sort of like his unofficial *fraa*. You know, got to check with the *fraa* of the house first!"

Jonas felt his face growing red, but he hardly cared at all. Shaking his head, he found himself laughing along with his friends.

"You know the saying, 'Happy wife, happy life,'" Samuel continued. Reaching out to slap Jonas on the arm, he asked, "When are you going to make it official, anyway?"

Jonas let out a deep breath and replied, "You know, I haven't decided yet. We're not that far along with things."

Samuel and Thomas both stopped laughing and simply stared at Jonas in total surprise.

"Do you mean..." Samuel cocked his head to one side as if he was trying to make sense of Jonas's words.

"You know, actually, if I'm honest, I think I love that *maedel*," Jonas blurted.

His friends couldn't have looked more shocked, and Jonas found their bewildered expressions quite humorous. Nodding, he went on to add, "I didn't think that any *maedel* was capable, but Abigail has managed to turn my head once and for all. She is the *maedel* for me, and I am proud to say that I'm no longer a confirmed bachelor."

"*Ach*, Jonas!" Thomas exclaimed once he found his voice. He stepped forward to give his friend a pat on the back as he declared, "I'm so happy for you!"

"Me, too!" Samuel threw in with a laugh. "I never thought I'd see the day."

Starting to feel uncomfortable with all the attention, Jonas pointed toward the outside and said, "How about we get out there and start moving those other boards in here. Now that the pens are built, I want to make some feed troughs."

Hurrying out into the sunshine, Jonas felt a mixture of discomfort and excitement. There was something nice about being the one who was on the receiving end of all the congratulations. It seemed like opening his heart to romance had truly been the best decision in every possible way.

"Mrs. Smoker!" Samuel called out to Jonas's mother, who was hanging the laundry out on the line, "You should be so proud...your little *bu* is getting married."

"What?" Barbara exclaimed, the towel that she had been folding dropped to the dirty ground. Paying no attention to her soiled laundry, she rushed over to their sides and asked, "Is this the truth?"

"*Ya*," Thomas piped up, "Jonas was just saying that he thinks Abigail might be the one."

Jonas felt absolutely humiliated, yet when his mother looked at him, silently questioning him, a smile crossed his lips as he nodded. She clapped her hands in delight and cried out, "Praise *Gott*! This is the day I have been praying for. I told her that I knew she was the one."

The comment splattered on Jonas's good mood like mud on a wall, marring his joy, and the smile disappeared from his lips. What did his mother mean that she told Abigail something about being *the one*? She and Abigail had been talking together behind his back? When did this happen? It felt like they had somehow been scheming together, and he didn't like the idea of being a pawn in their game.

Forcing himself to swallow the sudden bitter taste in his mouth, Jonas decided not to make a big deal of it. After all, it should come as no surprise to him that his mother and Abigail would talk. And, of course, his mother might say some awkward things. It didn't mean that Abigail was scheming behind his back...did it?

Turning back toward the pile of lumber, Jonas suggested, "How about we stop worrying about my love life and work on getting this stuff to the barn."

As much as Jonas tried not to dwell on his mother's revelation, it persistently and doggedly returned and nagged at him. He started to wonder if Abigail was truly all that she seemed. He could only hope that she didn't have a sinister, secret side that she was hiding from him!

Up in the buggy seat next to Pete, Abigail gripped the edge of the wooden seat so hard that her fingers were white. Her anger, though still in check, was just under control; it felt like she might break the wood in two with her bare hands.

The upcoming fork in the road could take one either left to Bishop Kauffman's house or right to Jonas's. At that moment, she was offering silent prayers, hoping that Jonas would have heard nothing that would make him think that she was a run-around. Their relationship was still so tender and fresh—news like that might be just what it took to destroy it entirely.

When Pete veered to the right, Abigail sat up straighter in her seat and looked at him in utter confusion.

"What are you doing?" she asked, her heart suddenly starting to pound furiously in her chest. "The bishop lives in the other direction!"

Ignoring her completely, Pete just urged his horse forward.

Reaching out to put a hand on his arm, Abigail urged him, "Pete, we're going the wrong way!"

Shrugging, Pete replied, "*Ach*, I don't think so. We're just taking a little longer route—it will loop back around so that we can see the bishop."

Abigail had been anxious to see Bishop Kauffman and then get back home. She wasn't prepared to be paraded across the entire Amish community, yet it seemed like that was exactly what Pete Zook intended to do! If they were to go by Jonas's house, it might destroy everything! What if he was to see her with Pete?

Not knowing what else to do, Abigail turned to Pete and declared, "Pete, I want to go home! I'll get to the bishop's house myself."

"*Nee*, Abigail," Pete assured her, his voice serious, but there was a definite twinkle of triumph in his eyes. "You want to make sure that we get this misunderstanding taken care of!" It was obvious that he was enjoying her discomfort. Abigail wasn't sure if he was doing it just to scare her or if he was truly planning to try and out her to Jonas.

Glancing at the passing scenery on the side of the road, Abigail wondered how badly she might get injured if she simply jumped off the moving buggy. She might break a few bones and get some scrapes, but at that point, she hardly cared. She couldn't believe that Pete was doing this to her.

"*Ach*, look!" Pete exclaimed as he pointed toward Jonas's approaching house. "It looks like Jonas is outside working! Why don't you yell out and call for him? I'm sure he'd be happy to see you greeting him."

Sitting back in the buggy, Abigail held her breath, hoping that Jonas was so busy with his work that he wouldn't notice her out driving with Pete Zook. What had started out as a perfect day was quickly turning into a nightmare.

Chapter Twelve

Jonas couldn't wipe the grin off his face as he nailed another board in place. Despite the hint of uncertainty his mother's words caused, he had chosen to ignore it and focused on the joy of his newfound romance instead. Now that he had Abigail in his life, it felt like everything had even more purpose and excitement than ever before—and he wasn't about to let that go simply because Abigail and his mother had spoken about him, disconcerting as it was.

"*Kumm* on, guys!" Jonas called out to Samuel and Thomas. "By the time Abigail gets here tonight, I want her to be shocked at all that we've gotten done."

"*Ach*, you're starting to sound like a taskmaster!" Samuel teased in reply. "We're not your slaves."

The sound of an approaching buggy drew

the trio's attention toward the road. Deep in his heart, Jonas found himself hoping that it might be Abigail headed in their direction. While he wasn't expecting to see her until that evening, it would sure be a good surprise if she were to show up early.

"*Ach*, it's just Pete Zook," Thomas commented with a shake of his head as the buggy drew closer into view. He laughed and said, "Wonder what impressive project he's off to go work on?"

Samuel chuckled and said, "Knowing that blowhard, he'd probably try to convince us he's going to build the next Eiffel tower right here in Morrissey County!"

The boys all laughed at the comment, but then Samuel stopped, and his face became serious as he asked, "Wait…isn't that Abigail riding with him?"

Jonas's heart stopped beating. *Abigail with Pete Zook? That's impossible!* He turned his attention toward the approaching buggy and felt his heart accelerate from stunned to tachycardic when he recognized that it was none other than his sweet Abigail perched up on the seat next to Pete. *What is this supposed to mean? How can Abigail be out riding with Pete when she knows I have feelings for her? We even have an understanding, yet here she is, parading past my house with another young man!* "I can't believe it!" Jonas muttered under his breath.

"*Nee*, it surely can't be!" Thomas returned with a shake of his head. "Abigail wouldn't do something like that!"

But Jonas had seen her with his own eyes. Shaking his head, he tossed down the hammer he had been carrying and declared, "I have to find out what's going on!" Rushing toward the road, Jonas called out, "Abigail!"

When he spoke her name, she turned around and looked directly at him. Jonas couldn't read her expression, but he hardly cared. Even though Pete was going too fast for her to say anything to Jonas, it didn't matter. It was obvious that she had betrayed him, and their relationship was finished. In that moment, Jonas experienced such intense heartbreak that he wished that he had never let himself care for Abigail Speicher at all. In fact, he wished that he had never met her.

As he strode back to the house, Jonas knew that the anguish and disappointment he was reeling from must surely be written all over his face. His friends looked at him with uncertainty, clearly unsure how to respond.

"*Ach*, Jonas. I am so sorry!" Samuel whispered,

looking down at the ground.

"Don't give up on her, Jonas!" Thomas pleaded with a vehement shake of his head, following along behind Jonas. "I know that Abigail wouldn't do something like that to you. She's a faithful *maedel*! And her heart belongs to *you*."

But the words were like an ant punching an elephant; they carried ridiculously little weight after what Jonas had seen. He had been betrayed by Abigail—she was nothing more than just a runaround, flitting from one young man to the next. The fact that he could be so easily deceived broke Jonas's heart in two.

Even with the distance between them, Abigail had been able to see the grief and disappointment on Jonas's face. He had been heartbroken when he saw her riding with Pete in his buggy—and understandably so. How terrible it must have looked to see her riding so closely to Pete right after Jonas had declared his love to her the previous night!

"Pete!" Abigail said assertively. She wanted to

chastise him and tear into him for what he had just done, but the words stuck in her throat, and she couldn't seem to dislodge them.

What point is there in even saying anything now? He has managed to do exactly what he intended; he's driven a wedge between me and Jonas—a wedge that may as well as weigh a million tons it is so immovable.

As he pranced his buggy back around toward Bishop Kauffman's house, looking like a cat who ate the canary, Abigail felt like she was on display to all and sundry. They passed dozens of Amish homes, many of the inhabitants out working in their yards and looking up in time to see her and Pete together. Abigail tried to hide her face with her hands, but she resigned herself to the fact that people probably still recognized her.

When they finally arrived at the bishop's house, the blinds were drawn, and there was no sign of life. Shrugging his shoulders, Pete announced, "Well, looks like no one is home." Without another word and wearing an expression of having not a care in the world, he turned the buggy back toward the road and drove on toward the Speicher home.

When they arrived at the house that Abigail shared with her mother, Pete turned to look at her;

he gave a malicious smirk as he flippantly said, "Sorry things didn't work out. I know you wanted to clear things up with the bishop...but I don't know that it would have helped anyway." His eyes narrowed and darkened as he menacingly warned, "Don't ever think you can turn me down for the likes of someone like Jonas Smoker."

Not even waiting for the buggy to come to a stop, Abigail turned in a sharp movement and jumped down from the seat. Her black shoes hit the driveway with a thud, and pain shot up her legs. She didn't care—she just wanted to escape from Pete. Tears were streaming down her face, sobs were racking her body, and all she wanted to do was take cover in the safety of her home.

Abigail ran up the porch and practically leaped into the house, slamming the door behind her and then locking it. Leaning her back against the door as she panted from the exertion, she gave in to her tears and wept bitterly. Her entire world had come crashing down.

"Abigail, is that you? Did you get my sugar—" Colette stepped into the front room and took in the condition of her youngest daughter. Sudden concern crossed her face and she exclaimed, "*Ach,* Abigail! What on earth has happened, *Liewi*?"

Hurrying over to her side, Colette put a hand on her daughter's shoulder, and Abigail threw herself into her mother's arms like a little child who had been hurt and craved comfort and reassurance that everything would be okay.

"*Ach, Maem!*" Abigail pressed her face against her mother's shoulder and let her tears soak the older woman's green dress. "My life is ruined! I saw Pete on the road, and he told me the silliest stories about gossip going around in town. He said that people were saying that I was a run-around, and he offered to take me to the bishop's house to clear it all up." Shaking her head, Abigail reached up to rub her pounding temple as she recalled the horrible truth. "He offered me a ride, and ignorant me took him up on his offer." Her sobs grew as she admitted, "He just used it as an opportunity to take me by Jonas's house and flaunt me with him on his buggy."

Colette's face grew even paler than usual, and she pulled back and held her arms on Abigail's shoulders. "Maybe Jonas didn't see you?" she suggested.

Shaking her head, Abigail plopped forward again and buried her face back in her mother's shoulder as she whispered, "*Nee*, he saw me. He looked right at me and called my name. I know that he must think terrible things about me. Jonas will never again want to have anything to do with me. I could see the heartbreak and confusion in his eyes."

Just verbalizing the whole despicable conundrum brought on yet another wave of sobs. The rug of hope for a future with Jonas had literally been pulled out from under her.

Still standing near the Smoker barn, Thomas watched as Jonas marched toward the pile of boards. The look on his face was one that Thomas had never seen on his friend: Jonas looked angry at the world, but more than anything else, he looked dejected and defeated. Grabbing one of the boards, Jonas lifted it up and then slammed it back down onto the pile.

"That two-timing *maedel*!" he snarled, shaking his head so hard that his felt hat fell to the ground. "That *maedel* and her devious ways. I knew that I was stupid to look at a woman."

"Jonas." Thomas stepped forward and shook

his head. "I just can't believe that Abi would do this to you. Not after she told you that she cares about you! Just a few minutes ago, you were practically ready to marry her. I'm sure it's all a big misunderstanding. Don't let Pete Zook mess it all up!"

Thomas opened his mouth to elaborate on how Abigail had told him that Jonas was the only man that could ever have a place in her heart, but the words got stuck in his throat as he thought, *I can't tell him. Jonas will surely hate me if I tell him I tried to pursue her—even if it was done in innocence!*

"Sorry, but I've got to go and check on the crops," Jonas declared, crossing his arms defiantly against his chest. "Let's call it a day. You all feel free to just go home."

With that, Jonas turned and marched toward the section of the farm where the crops filled the fields. Thomas wasn't sure, but he thought that he saw tears in his old friend's eyes. As soon as Jonas disappeared, Thomas turned to Samuel as if looking for his other friend's opinion.

Samuel looked totally stunned. He shrugged and said, "*Ach*, I don't believe that Abigail would outright cheat on Jonas. Do you? She seems to care about him quite a bit!"

"*Ya,*" Thomas agreed. "She sure does." Looking after Jonas's slumped but disappearing form, he knew that he had to do something. Standing up straighter, he turned to Samuel and declared, "I may not be able to do much, but I've got to do something to help them. I'm going to go talk to Abigail and her *maem.* I'll get to the bottom of this one way or another."

Samuel supportively responded, "*Ya,* that sounds like a *gut* idea."

Setting the boards aside, Thomas hurried to hitch up his buggy. The sooner he could talk to Abigail Speicher, the better.

Chapter Thirteen

A fresh onslaught of tears assaulted Abigail as she sat on the edge of her bed. She had been crying off and on ever since Pete dropped her off at her home. Every time she thought she had just successfully pulled herself together, she would remember the whole incident and the floodgates would open. Reaching up to wipe her eyes, she wondered, *how did things turn sour so quickly?*

"Why *Gott*?" she whispered as she pulled a handkerchief out of her dress pocket and held it up to her eyes. "Why would You allow this to happen? Why would You let Jonas fall in love with me, only to allow it all to fall apart so quickly?"

It simply didn't make sense. It felt like she had been somehow betrayed by the Lord Himself. Surely if He cared for her, He would have prevented the day's awful events from taking place.

Gathering a calming breath, she reminded herself that her future was in the hands of the Lord, and regardless of how she might feel about the outcome, He could help to direct her path.

Shaking her head, Abigail struggled again to understand all that had happened in the last few hours.

"Abigail!" The sound of her mother calling from downstairs made her sit up straighter. "Abi, *kumm* down. We have some company."

Gathering all her strength, she dabbed at her swollen red eyes and made her way toward the bedroom door. She didn't want to see anyone, but she knew that if it wasn't important, her mother wouldn't have called for her.

Making her way to the steps, Abigail held her breath for fear of what might come next. She carefully made her way down, but she felt sick to her stomach and didn't know if she could make it to her mother's side without vomiting. She knew that her face must be red and blotchy and her eyes tear-stained, but she couldn't muster enough energy to make herself presentable in the half-bathroom. Whoever had stopped by would just have to put up with her in all her misery.

Rounding the corner and stepping into the sitting room, Abigail was surprised to see that Thomas Yoder had come by for a visit.

"Thomas," she muttered, quickly diverting her gaze down to the floor. "What are you doing here?"

Thomas was standing in the doorway, confusion etched on his face while he twirled his felt hat in his hands. "Abigail, I don't know what happened today, but that entire situation with Pete Zook has started a mess. Jonas is so upset, and he's thinking the worst possible things."

Each word that came out of Thomas's mouth only made her feel worse and confirmed her suspicions that Jonas would likely consider their budding relationship over.

"Before I try to convince him that things weren't how they seemed, I wanted to *kumm* by and make sure that I'm right," Thomas explained. "Why were you out riding with Pete? He's not courting you now, is he?"

Shaking her head furiously, Abigail welcomed the chance to finally convince someone of the truth. "*Nee*, never! I would never date him. He tricked me into riding with him. He told me that there were rumors about me riding with other young men and offered me a ride to the bishop's house to clear my *gut* name. It turned out it was only a chance to run my reputation through the mud as payback for turning him down."

Anger washed over Thomas's face, and he shook his head. "*Ach*, I should have known that he was doing something like that! Pete Zook has always been a pain. And since the bishop is his *daed's* best friend, he thinks he can get away with anything!"

Snapping her fingers together, Colette interjected, "I think I'm going to go get my shawl. Thomas, if you don't mind going on and taking me to the Smoker house, I'd like to have a talk with Barbara. It seems like this might be a *gut* time for two widows to band together to help their *kinner* out!"

Nodding in obvious relief, Thomas assured her, "That would be no problem at all." Turning his gaze toward Abigail, he added, "You should *kumm*, too. Jonas is brokenhearted. You need to help him get this all sorted out. You surely understand why he's so confused. He needs *you* to tell him the truth."

Her exhaustion and the emotions and events of the day weighed heavily on Abigail. She had invested so much trying to pursue Jonas, only to have it end so badly. She was finished, running on dry, empty. Shaking her head slowly, she said, "*Nee.* I'll stay here. If Jonas still wants me, then he'll have to *kumm* to me."

Watching her mother and Thomas prepare to leave, Abigail yearned for Jonas to come to see her. But deep in her heart, it seemed very unlikely. Jonas had never been one to try to fight for her affection, and she was sure that now he was less likely than ever to put his heart on the line for someone he wasn't sure he could trust.

Walking through the knee-high fields of corn, Jonas swallowed hard against the gigantic lump in his throat. Never would he have thought that things with Abigail would turn out this way.

"But you should have known," he muttered to himself as he kicked the toe of his boot against a clod of dirt on the ground.

Yes, Jonas should have known how easily things could turn from good to bad. Hadn't he seen that with his father? One day, they had been a happy family, enjoying each other's company while working the land, and then the next, the man who had held their family together was gone. Life was uncertain.

"You're better off not depending on anyone else," Jonas whispered, a sob catching in his throat. "No amount of love or joy is worth the risk of heartbreak."

While Jonas had always been happy with his freedom in the past, he now found the idea of spending his future alone terribly depressing and lonely. He was going to have to learn to enjoy it again, though, because that was best. Abigail's behavior with Pete Zook had proven that women were unreliable.

"Jonas!" Thomas's familiar voice made Jonas look up in time to see his friend taking long strides in his direction.

Jonas hoped that the tears that had moistened his eyes weren't noticeable. Forcing himself to look up and meet his friend's gaze, Jonas wished that Thomas had simply left and stayed away. He didn't have the capacity to deal with visiting or talking.

"Thomas...what are you still doing here?" he forced himself to ask. "Why aren't you at home? You need to go home. I just need some time alone to process what happened with Abigail."

Stepping closer to him, Thomas's face looked pale. He shook his head slowly and said, "I need to talk to you about Abigail."

"I'm afraid I don't feel like talking," Jonas replied curtly. "I just want to be left alone for a little while. You go on home to your *familye…*"

"Abigail didn't do anything wrong!" Thomas persisted.

His words caused a scornful laugh to roil in Jonas's belly, but he bit it back. Raising his eyebrows, he said, "Thomas, I appreciate you trying to help me, but I don't think that there's any point in attempting to make excuses for her. Abigail was out on a buggy with Pete Zook. It's pretty easy to see what's going on."

"*Nee,*" Thomas insisted. "I went by her house and talked to her. She says that she was tricked. She says that Pete told her a bunch of lies and tricked her into riding with him."

Hope sprinkled over Jonas's shriveled heart. *Can it be true? Is it possible that she really was just tricked into riding with Pete and wasn't on a date?* But Jonas brushed aside the hope in self-preservation from being hurt further.

"That doesn't matter," he mumbled. "I'm sure she would say anything to excuse her behavior."

"She only has eyes for you, Jonas. No matter what you think or what you see, believe me. It's the truth!"

How could Thomas know such things? He was being ridiculous to think that just because Abigail seemed nice that she might not have a dubious secret side. Plenty of girls were known for being unfaithful. Who was to say that Abigail wasn't one of them? Perhaps she just liked the chase and got a thrill from tricking young men into falling for her and then led them on as a sort of game. So many terrible thoughts filled Jonas's mind, and every bit of confidence that he had ever had in Abigail evaporated.

"Abigail is true to you, Jonas!" Thomas asserted.

Raising an eyebrow, Jonas bluntly asked, "And how would you know that?"

"Because I tried to get her to let me court her!" Thomas exclaimed seemingly before he even knew the words were coming out his mouth. He held his friend's gaze with a face that was quickly turning red.

"You did what?" Jonas asked, his face growing pale as reality hit him. His own friend had double-crossed him as well?

Taking a step forward, Thomas hurried to explain, "It was before you two had any sort of agreement. It was weeks ago—right after we first started working together. I enjoyed being around her so much, and she was just such a unique *maedel*! How many other *maed* do you know who look beautiful while swinging a hammer? I told her that I'd like to court her, but she turned me down."

Jonas listened carefully to every word. He scrunched his face up in a frown, trying to make sense of why Abigail would turn Thomas down if she was going to go riding with a young man as repulsive as Pete Zook.

"She told me that she wouldn't date me... because she only has room in her heart for one *mann*. And that one *mann* is you, Jonas Smoker. I even warned her that you vowed to be a bachelor for life, but she said she didn't care. She would wait for you."

The words left Jonas stunned. He stared at his friend, speechless. "Sh-she said w-what?" he finally managed to ask.

"She only cares for you, Jonas," Thomas assured him with a sigh. "And I'm sorry that I tried to pursue her, but it was without realizing you two were even interested in each other." Looking down at the ground, Thomas said, "I can't promise you much, but I would stake my life on the fact that Abigail Speicher is only interested in you. And she has been since she first met you."

A torrent of emotions washed over Jonas all at once. Could he actually believe that this was true? Had Abigail really said such things? Yet, he knew that Thomas would never lie.

Sniffling to keep his emotions in check, Jonas asked huskily, "Where is she now?"

Shrugging, Thomas explained, "She said that she was going to stay home while her *maem* came here to visit with your *maem*. She said that if you really cared about her, then you would go after her."

Of course he would go after her! What other choice was there? As much as he tried to push her away early on, Jonas had grown to love Abigail more than he ever even imagined loving another person. When he thought she chose Pete Zook over him, he had been shattered. But now that Thomas had vouched for her, he would be a fool to let another minute go by letting her think that things were over between them. Without another thought, he nodded and said, "I'm going to talk to her now!"

∞ ∞ ∞

Bursting into the house and hardly caring if he was interrupting his mother's conversation, Jonas found Barbara and Colette standing inside the doorway, chatting. The two women were acting like they were lifelong friends.

Looking up in surprise, Barbara said, "*Ach*, Jonas! You're just the person that I wanted to see. You've got to go talk to Abigail!"

"*Ya*," Colette threw in with a nod, her pale face looking more weathered with concern than usual. "Abigail is beside herself. She never meant to hurt you."

Shaking his head, Jonas held up a hand and hurried to assure them. "Don't worry—that's exactly what I'm planning to do right now. I was just coming in to tell you that I'm leaving and to go on with the plans for our supper together."

Barbara looked up at the ceiling and whispered a quiet prayer of thanks. Colette grabbed onto the back of a nearby chair and seemed to be gasping for breath. When she had finally collected herself,

Abigail's mother turned her attention back to Jonas and said, "What happened today was truly a mistake. That awful Pete Zook has been a pain ever since Abigail first agreed to go riding with him. I'm afraid that it was my fault because I pushed her to date him…but I had no idea that he'd be so hard to deal with…"

"It's all right, Mrs. Speicher," Jonas assured her, hoping to stop her in the middle of her story. At that moment, he was only interested in getting back to Abigail. "I'm not worried about Pete Zook."

"*Ya*, but Abigail is," Colette insisted. "She's sure that he's ruined her reputation once and for all. She thinks that you will never speak to her again and that her entire standing in the *gmay* is destroyed."

Jonas wished that he had responded differently when he saw Abigail with Pete. Surely, she had been able to see the disappointment on his face. But, in that moment, rather than consider other possible reasons, he had only believed the worst.

"I can't do anything about the *gmay*…" Jonas started in reply, but his mother's face stopped him. She and Colette looked at each other with naughty smiles that most certainly promised the two widows had cooked up some sort of devious plan.

"We actually think you can," Colette announced, and Barbara stepped forward to put an arm around her son's shoulders. "Just let us explain."

Chapter Fourteen

bigail couldn't remember a time in her life when she had ever felt more alone. Yes, it had been difficult once her father died, but that was nothing compared to the shame and humiliation that she now felt mixed with her sorrow.

"How could this have happened?" she asked into the empty yard as she walked out toward the barn. Abigail had done everything in her power to remain a good, well-behaved girl who never stepped outside the lines of the *Ordnung*. She had tried her best to remain virtuous and honest, never giving her family a care or concern. But now, due to another's lies and deception, she had lost it all in a heartbeat.

"All because of gossip and scandal, my life is ruined," Abigail exclaimed, throwing her hands up toward the sky.

"*Gott*, why would You allow me to suffer so much when I've done nothing wrong?" she asked.

As soon as the words crossed her lips, Abigail instantly felt guilty. How dare she complain so much? Jesus had suffered much worse for doing nothing wrong. In the grand scheme of things, the Lord had blessed her abundantly. She would trust that God had a plan through this recent turn of events.

"Maybe Jonas isn't the right one for me," she whispered as she leaned her shoulder against the side of the barn. The thought shocked her to the core. She had been so anxious to try to get to know Jonas and to fulfill her mother's biggest wish that Abigail did little in seeking the Lord's will about Jonas being right for her.

What if Jonas wasn't a part of the plan for her life? What if she had been rushing ahead outside of the Lord's plan for her?

Instantly, Abigail felt guilty for her lack of faith and for forgetting about God almost entirely in her pursuit of Jonas. She had started out with the best of intentions, but her focus slowly turned toward only accomplishing her mission, regardless of who might stand in her way.

Marriage to Jonas had become a sort of idol, and maybe the Lord was using this situation to turn her eyes back toward Him.

Closing her eyes, she soaked in the warmth of the sun that shone down on her prayer kapp. "I surrender this situation to You, *Gott*," she whispered softly into the afternoon air. "It's up to You what happens now. If Jonas doesn't *kumm* back for me, then I will take it as a sign that it wasn't meant to be…and that You have something better in mind."

As she whispered the words, tears began to spill down her cheeks. They were tears of relief rather than sadness. By putting things into the Lord's hands, she could at least depend on the course of her life finally going in the right direction. No matter how difficult the situation might be, nothing was too big for the Lord to change when He was working with a willing heart.

"Abigail?" The voice was so soft that for a moment she wondered if it might be a dream. "Abigail?" it repeated, and a gentle but firm hand patted her on the shoulder.

Abigail turned around in surprise. She thought she might fall over when she found Jonas standing directly behind her, an awkward and somewhat ashamed look on his face.

Reaching up, Jonas took off the black felt hat and began to wring it in his hands. He looked utterly out of place, yet Abigail was so happy to see him that it took every ounce of restraint that she possessed not to throw herself into his arms.

"Jonas." She whispered his name around the lump in her throat. Suddenly considering all that he must be thinking, she rushed to say, "Jonas, I am so sorry for the way that things turned out today! I am so sorry for any confusion or misunderstanding..."

Jonas began to shake his head and held up a finger to hush her. Stepping closer so that he could look her directly in the face, his own voice sounded husky as he said, "*Nee*, I'm the one who needs to apologize. I'm sorry for doubting you." She could see his eyes dart back to the ground before he looked back at her, and Abigail was sure that it was taking every bit of courage that he had to look her in the eye as he spoke.

"Abigail, when I saw you with Pete, I had terrible thoughts. I was ready to call it all off entirely...until Thomas reminded me of what an amazing, faithful *maedel* you are." Biting down on his lip, he said, "I thought that you had left me for

Pete…and it broke my heart. Abigail, do you really love me?"

The question seemed loaded, but Abigail didn't care. She was ready to reveal her deepest feelings to this dear man with whom she hoped to spend the rest of her days. "*Ya*, Jonas. I love you—more than anything or anyone else on earth. There is no one that I'd even consider being with other than you!"

Reaching to put a finger on her cheek, Jonas stepped a little closer as he promised, "Abigail, you've managed to do something no other *maedel* ever could. You managed to get my attention, and you managed to win my heart. I love you so much that I would even give up my plans for the farm just to have you. You mean the world to me now. I don't just want to say that we're going to work toward courting…I want us to actually be a couple. I want us to get married and live the rest of our lives together until *Gott* calls one of us home."

Feeling her eyes filling with happy tears, Abigail gladly stepped into Jonas's embrace when he reached out and encircled her in his arms. Pressed tightly against his body, she breathed in the fresh scent of pine shavings and hay.

She took a step back, and she gasped as his lips

found hers; the two of them shared a quick but sweet true love's kiss.

Nestling against his chest once more, Abigail felt like she was at home. How wonderful it was that God had managed to turn a bad situation around, bringing something beautiful out of what had seemed like an impossible ordeal.

Remembering Pete, Abigail stood up straighter and looked directly at Jonas. Horror filled her voice as she asked, "But what about Pete, Jonas? After what he did today, who's not to say that he won't try something similar again? He may even try to convince the *gmay* that he and I are courting and that I'm being unfaithful to him when I'm out with you!"

Chuckling under his breath, Jonas put his hand against her neck and softly rubbed it as he announced, "Don't you worry about Pete Zook. Our *maems* have already talked to me about a plan to silence that boy once and for all!"

While Abigail had no clue what that might be, in that moment, she didn't care. Everything seemed right in the world, and she had no trouble being certain that the Lord, even if it was through some meddling mothers, would take care of any problem that might arise in their lives.

∞ ∞ ∞

Standing by the picket fence in his front yard, Abron Kauffman listened as Pete Zook recounted the details of the ride he had taken with Abigail Speicher earlier that day. As the young man explained all that happened, Abron began to feel a sense of pride well up within him.

"So, like you had told me, if she was bold enough to go on a ride with me for any reason, then it was something that Jonas Smoker should see for himself...along with everyone that might be on the roadside." Pete smirked as he pulled a nail out of his pocket and worked to repair a weak spot in the fence.

"Well, well." The bishop nodded his head as he said, "I'm not sure how I exactly feel about some parts of your story...such as you misleading her, but..." Tugging on his beard, he thought it over carefully before admitting, "*Ach,* I don't see that you actually lied. Surely, nothing went against the *Ordnung.*"

Smirking, Pete replied, "I'm pretty sure that Jonas Smoker won't be any competition for me now. I only got a glimpse at him, but he looked shocked, to say the least. I'd say he'll be back to hiding away at that farm and just focusing on raising livestock."

Raising an eyebrow at the thought of it, Abron gave another nod as he commented, "It's hard to believe he'd do anything else."

The sound of an approaching buggy made them both glance toward the road. Raising a hand, Abron instinctively started to wave before he could even see who was coming their direction.

"*Gude daag*, Bishop Kauffman!" a man's voice called out. "*Gude daag*, Pete Zook!"

Pete's face instantly turned ashen, and he dropped the hammer that he was holding to the ground in shock. Squinting his eyes against the late afternoon sun, Abron felt his own heart leap within his chest when he recognized that the passengers in the buggy were none other than Jonas Smoker and Abigail Speicher herself.

"Abigail and I are courting now, Bishop!" Jonas announced as he slowed his buggy down to a trot. "Be prepared, because we're probably going to be looking to get married very soon." Smiling as boldly as he had ever smiled before, Jonas asked, "Is there anything we can get you in town? We're headed that way right now!"

Abron opened his mouth, but no words would come out. How could this have happened? He felt utterly foolish that his entire scheme had fallen apart.

Looking his archnemesis directly in the eye, Jonas asked, "Pete, what about you?"

When Pete didn't answer, either, Jonas pulled the reins and declared, "Looks like that's a no. *Mach's gut*, you two!"

With a flick of his wrist, Jonas urged the horse forward and sent his buggy on down the road, leaving the two men standing and staring in horror.

"How on earth…how did…that scumbag!" Pete exclaimed as he kicked his foot against one of the posts of the fence, only to start hopping around in pain when he stubbed his toe.

Paying no attention to Pete, Abron stepped forward and stared after the young couple. His eyes narrowed as he watched them scoot closer together, their heads almost touching as they talked.

"Just wait, Jonas Smoker," Abron whispered between gritted teeth. "This may not be the last time that you double-cross me…but it will be the last time you get away with it!"

Turning back to his neighbor, Abron grimaced when he noticed just how crooked Pete had left his supposedly repaired fence. The boy certainly was no carpenter, and viewing his work made Abron that much more frustrated.

Holding an ice cream cone in one hand, Jonas directed the buggy back toward the Smoker home, where his mother and Colette were waiting on them. Turning to look at Abigail, he said, "Well, I think we have been seen by almost every *familye* in the *gmay*."

Abigail snickered as she took another lick of her ice cream. Glancing at Jonas out of the corner of her eye, Abigail said, "You certainly gave it your best effort. I think you about tracked down everyone who was in the town and drove by the homes of others who weren't in town."

Grinning broadly, Jonas nodded and said, "That was my goal."

Reaching out an arm, he directed Abigail to scoot closer to him, and he encircled her with his arm. There was something so refreshing and nice about having her there with him, tucked against his body.

"*Danki* for doing all this for me." Abigail spoke seriously as she took the last bite of her ice cream. "I sure do appreciate it. Everyone now knows who I'm courting, and there will be no doubts."

"There's never going to be any doubts," Jonas assured her, "because next, I'm going to make you my *fraa*...and then I'll never have to ever worry about losing you again. Unless something terrible happens."

As soon as the words slipped off his tongue, Jonas wished that he hadn't spoken them. He hated the idea of losing another person too early in life. And yet, in that moment, he realized that Abigail would be worth any heartache that life ever sent their way.

"*Danki*," Jonas said as he leaned over to kiss her on the cheek. "*Danki* for loving me."

While they knew that their mothers were waiting for them to get back to the Smoker homestead, they didn't rush. Instead, they let the horse meander along slowly, basking in their time together. Thankfully, it would be the first of many days that the couple would spend side by side.

<h1 style="text-align:center">*Epilogue*</h1>

Scooting her chair closer to the bed where her little boy lay back against his pillow, Abigail reached out and stroked a strand of hair back from his face.

"So, that's how your *daed* and I got together," she explained, finishing the bedtime story that had quickly turned into a very long tale.

Ten-year-old Steven Smoker sat up a little straighter in bed and stared at his mother, trying to make sense of everything that he had just been told. "But what about Pete Zook? Did he ever cause any more problems?"

Laughing at the memory of him, Abigail shook her head slowly and said, "*Nee*, he certainly did not. I think your *daed* put him in his place once and for all when he took me out on our first buggy ride as a courting couple. Pete never came around again. And he was so humiliated and stunned he never said anything to anyone, either. A few months later, he went to stay with a *kossin* in Indiana, where he ended up meeting a *maedel* that he married. I think they're still in Indiana."

Secretly, Abigail couldn't help but pity whatever poor woman might have found herself married to that bumbling, boastful bully of a man.

"And the bishop?" Steven pressed. "Does he still hate *Daed*?"

Cocking her head to one side, Abigail tried to determine just how much she should tell her little boy. "*Ach*, I don't know about that," she replied. "I don't think they are what you might call friends, but they do tolerate each other. He's no one to be concerned about now. I doubt he ever thinks about our *familye*."

Leaning back in bed, Steven snuggled down under the blankets and asked, "How soon after you started courting did you and *daed* get married?"

Letting her mind travel back in time, Abigail remembered the rush that there was to get a wedding performed after her mother's health went downhill. Tears filled her eyes as she admitted, "Not very long at all. Around two months. Your *Groossmammi* Colette wanted to see me married to a *gut mann* before she died, so we had a very small ceremony. It wasn't what I had hoped for, but at least she got her final wish… *Groossmammi* Colette died the following week." Rubbing her son's forehead, she added, "Hopefully, you can have a much bigger, more traditional wedding when your time comes."

Scrunching his face up into a frown, Steven looked almost repulsed as he admitted, "I can't imagine that I'll ever actually get married. It's going to have to be a mighty special *maedel* if I ever do!"

Chuckling at his comment, Abigail bent over to give him a kiss on the forehead as she pulled herself to her feet. Smiling at him, she said, "*Gude nacht, Liewer*. Get some rest."

Nodding his head, Steven smiled as he turned over on his stomach and closed his eyes.

Watching him from the doorway, Abigail was mesmerized. Sometimes, it was so hard to imagine that the Lord had blessed them with such a sweet, goodhearted little boy. Of course, she and Jonas would have been so excited to have daughters, but it seemed that the Lord had only planned for them to have boys—and she was grateful for Steven and his elder brothers.

"He's something special, isn't he, our youngest?" Jonas whispered as he stepped up behind his wife and put his chin on her shoulder.

Nodding ever so slightly, Abigail leaned her head against his as she said, "*Ya*, he sure is. We were blessed beyond what we could ever deserve when the Lord gave him to us."

Pulling the bedroom door shut so that her little boy could sleep, Abigail turned to her husband and whispered, "I think we were blessed in many ways."

As Jonas leaned down to give her a kiss, Abigail closed her eyes and let her mind travel back to the time when they had first met. They had encountered so many difficult situations and so many challenges, yet the Lord saw them through them all. She truly could not be a happier woman.

Kissing his wife tenderly, Jonas enveloped her in his arms and pulled her close against him. After fifteen years of marriage, it felt like they had been together a lifetime, yet having her so near still made his heart beat erratically. Closing his eyes and breathing in the smell of her rose-scented hair, Jonas said a silent prayer of thanks.

The Lord had been good to them. All of Jonas's plans for the farm had continued to develop and grow into reality, regardless of his marital status. Being married, he just had someone else to support him in his wild dreams and work by his side.

Pulling back from his wife, he looked at her as he admitted, "I remember before the two of us met, my *maem* was trying to convince me that it was important to have a *fraa*. I had every kind of excuse not to think about marriage, but she told me that I would miss out on so much by staying alone. I almost did miss out. But, thanks to you and *Gott* above, I didn't. Thanks to you, I got to experience the skipping of my heart when I saw you walking toward me during our wedding ceremony. I got to bask in the awe of holding each of our *buwe* for the first time. I have been able to share everything with you…and I wouldn't give any of it up for anything that the single life could have offered."

Smiling softly, Abigail whispered, "It's *gut* to hear you say things like that sometimes."

Wrapping his arms around her, Jonas picked his wife up and carried her across the hardwood floor. He planned to keep reminding her just how special she was to him every day for the rest of their time together. Until the Lord called one of them home, he was going to make it his goal to love and appreciate Abigail just as she deserved to be treated. He only hoped that it was a very long time until they had to part ways for their eternal home.

∞ ∞ ∞

Find out more of what happens to the women of Morrissey County as they search for love and acceptance.

Sarah (The Amish of Morrissey County Prequel)
Morrissey County, 1979
Sarah Kauffman has always abided by the Ordnung, and not only because her father happens to be the town's bishop and would, she feels, disown her if she didn't. But when her mother passes away, she longs to escape the clutches of her father and run away to the Englisch world. When her father wants her to marry someone she doesn't love, Sarah becomes even more desperate

to leave.

Jacob Renno, on the other hand, is happy with life on his farm. It keeps him so busy that the older bachelor has no time for love, but on lonely nights, he finds himself longing for a companion.

When Sarah and Jacob meet, there's an instant connection, but things get complicated. Jacob offers to help Sarah with her dilemma, but Bishop Kaufmann insists that she obey his wishes. Will Sarah run off to join the Englisch, or will the handsome farmer give her pause? Will her father disown her or give her his blessing?

Sadie (The Amish of Morrissey County Book One)
Morrissey County, 1999
Sadie Renno has never liked being Amish. Perhaps she inherited her mother, Sarah's, desire to leave the Amish. She saw one magazine of American culture when she was young and knew that was the life for her.

Aaron Miller, one of the town's most devout Amish community members, has always had an eye for Sadie Renno. He has spent as much time imagining their wedding as she has spent imagining her life in the city, but Sadie has no desire to be with a man who represents all that she is trying to escape.

Sadie meets someone with a car who is willing to whisk her away, but when Aaron learns that Sadie may leave the community, he does everything in his power to show her that she should stay. Will Aaron be able to lure her away from the city's lights? Or will Sadie manage to do what her mother couldn't?

Bridget (The Amish of Morrissey
County Book Two)
Morrissey County, 2000

Bridget Miller, the sister of devout Amish community member Aaron Miller, returns from life amongst the Englisch to a guarded Aaron who isn't sure he can trust her and doesn't want her affecting his happy life. He is determined to protect his family from Bridget's influence.

Steven Smoker wants nothing more than to take over his father's farm. However, his father refuses to leave the farm to a bachelor. Steven must marry an Amish girl or forfeit the farm. He begins to lose hope since Bridget Miller, the only girl he's ever loved, left the Amish years ago.

Steven runs into Bridget unexpectedly and learns that she wishes to return to the Amish! Will Steven be able to accept and trust Bridget despite her past? Will others in the community welcome her or shun her?0

Eliza (The Amish of Morrissey County Book Four)
Morrissey County, 2022

Eliza Miller is keen on the Englisch life. She got a job in a large real estate company and worked her way up to being the boss's secretary. The more she gets to know Englischers, the more she desires to break free of the shackles of her Amish community.

Andrew Blythe has built up and sold several businesses since he was in high school. Now, he's at the helm of a profitable real estate company. Still, he wonders if there's more to life than making money.

Eliza takes Andrew to meet her Amish relatives, and he begins to imagine a different life for himself. However, when Bishop Kauffman discovers Andrew's hidden secret, he sets his sights on keeping his great-granddaughter from marrying Andrew. Will he succeed in meddling in his family's love affairs one last time? Or can Eliza and Andrew overcome the obstacles in their way and forge a new path?

Thank you, readers!

Thank you for reading this book. It is important to me to share my stories with you and that you enjoy them. May I ask a favor of you? If you enjoyed this book, would you please take a moment to leave a review on Amazon and/or Goodreads? Thank you for your support!

Also, each week, I send my readers updates about my life as well as information about my new releases, freebies, promos, and book recommendations. If you're interested in receiving my weekly newsletter, please go to newsletter.sylviaprice.com, and it will ask you for your email. As a thank-you, you will receive several FREE exclusive short stories that aren't available for purchase!

Blessings,
Sylvia

The Origins of Cardinal Hill is the prequel to the Amish of Cardinal Hill series. Each book is a stand-alone read, but to make the most of the series, you should consider reading them in order.

A Promised Tomorrow (The Yoder Family Saga Prequel)

Available for FREE on Amazon

The Yoder Family Saga follows widow Miriam Yoder and her four unmarried daughters, Megan, Rebecca, Josephine, and Lillian, as they discover God's plans for them and the hope He provides for a happy tomorrow.

The Yoder women struggle to survive after Jeremiah Yoder succumbs to a battle with cancer. The family risks losing their farm and their livelihood. They are desperate to find a way to keep going. Will Miriam and her daughters be able to work together to keep their family afloat? Will God pull through for them and provide for them in their time of need?

A Promised Tomorrow is the prequel to the Yoder Family Saga. Join the Yoder women through their journey of loss and hope for a better future. Each book is a stand-alone read, but to make the most of the series, you should consider reading them in order. Start reading this sweet Amish romance today that will take you on a rollercoaster of emotions as you're welcomed into the life of the Yoder family.

The Christmas Cards: An Amish Holiday Romance

Lucy Yoder is a young Amish widow who recently lost the love of her life, Albrecht. As Christmas approaches, she dreads what was once her favorite holiday, knowing that this Christmas was supposed to be the first one she and Albrecht shared together. Then, one December morning, Lucy discovers a Christmas card from an anonymous sender on her doorstep. Lucy receives more cards, all personal, all tender, all comforting. Who in the shadows is thinking of her at Christmas?

Andy Peachey was born with a rare genetic disorder. Coming to grips with his predicament makes him feel a profound connection to Lucy Yoder. Seeking meaning in life, he uses his talents to give Christmas cheer. Will Andy's efforts touch Lucy's heart and allow her to smile again? Or will Lucy, herself, get in his way?

The Christmas Cards is a story of loss and love and the ability to find yourself again in someone else.

The Christmas Arrival: An Amish Holiday Romance

Rachel Lapp is a young Amish woman who is the daughter of the community's bishop. She is in the midst of planning the annual Christmas Nativity play when newcomer Noah Miller arrives in town to spend Christmas with his cousins. Encouraged by her father to welcome the new arrival, Rachel asks Noah to be a part of the Nativity.

Despite Rachel's engagement to Samuel King, a local farmer, she finds herself irrevocably drawn to Noah and his carefree spirit. Reserved and slightly shy, Noah is hesitant to get involved in the play, but an unlikely friendship begins to develop between Rachel and Noah, bringing with it unexpected problems, including a seemingly harmless prank with life-threatening consequences that require a Christmas miracle.

Will Rachel honor her commitment to Samuel, or will Noah win her affections?

Join these characters on what is sure to be a heartwarming holiday adventure! Instead of waiting for each part to be released, enjoy the entire Christmas Arrival series at once!

Amish Love Through The Seasons (The Complete Series)

Featuring many of the beloved characters from Sylvia Price's bestseller, The Christmas Arrival, as well as a new cast of characters, Amish Love Through the Seasons centers around a group of teenagers as they find friendship, love, and hope in the midst of trials. ***This special boxed set includes the entire series, plus a bonus companion story, "Hope for Hannah's Love."***

Tragedy strikes a small Amish community outside of Erie, Pennsylvania when Isaiah Fisher, a widower and father of three, is involved in a serious accident. When his family is left scrambling to pick up the pieces, the community unites to help the single father, but the hospital bills keep piling up. How will the family manage?

Mary Lapp, a youth in the community, decides to take up Isaiah's cause. She enlists the help of other teenagers to plant a garden and sell the produce. While tending to the garden, new relationships develop, but old ones are torn apart. With tensions mounting, will the youth get past their disagreements in order to reconcile and produce fruit? Will they each find love? Join them on their adventure through the seasons!

Included in this set are all the popular titles:
Seeds of Spring Love
Sprouts of Summer Love
Fruits of Fall Love
Waiting for Winter Love
"Hope for Hannah's Love" (a bonus companion short story)

Jonah's Redemption (Book 1)

Available for FREE on Amazon

Jonah has lost his community, and he's struggling to get by in the English world. He yearns for his Amish roots, but his past mistakes keep him from returning home.

Mary Lou is recovering from a medical scare. Her journey has impressed upon her how precious life is, so she decides to go on rumspringa to see the world.

While in the city, Mary Lou meets Jonah. Unable to understand his foul attitude, especially towards her, she makes every effort to share her faith with him. As she helps him heal from his past, an attraction develops.

Will Jonah's heart soften towards Mary Lou? What will God do with these two broken people?

Elijah: An Amish Story Of Crime And Romance

He's Amish. She's not. Each is looking for a change. What happens when God brings them together?

Elijah Troyer is eighteen years old when he decides to go on a delayed Rumspringa, an Amish tradition when adolescents venture out into the world to decide whether they want to continue their life in the Amish culture or leave for the ways of the world. He has only been in the city for a month when his life suddenly takes a strange twist.

Eve Campbell is a young woman in trouble with crime lords, and they will do anything to stop her from talking. After a chance encounter, Elijah is drawn into Eve's world at the same time she is drawn into his heart. He is determined to help Eve escape from the grips of her past, but his Amish upbringing has not prepared him for the dangers he encounters as he tries to pull Eve from her chaotic world and into his peaceful one.

Will Elijah choose to return to the safety of his family, or will the ways of the world sink their hooks into him? Do Elijah and Eve have a chance at a future together? Find out in this action-packed standalone novel.

Songbird Cottage Beginnings (Pleasant Bay Prequel)

Available for FREE on Amazon

Set on Canada's picturesque Cape Breton Island, this book is perfect for those who enjoy new beginnings and countryside landscapes.

Sam MacAuley and his wife Annalize are total opposites. When Sam wants to leave city life in Halifax to get a plot of land on Cape Breton Island, where he grew up, his wife wants nothing to do with his plans and opts to move herself and their three boys back to her home country of South Africa.

As Sam settles into a new life on his own, his friend Lachlan encourages him to get back into the dating scene. Although he meets plenty of women, he longs to find the one with whom he wants to share the rest of his life. Will Sam ever meet "the one"?

Get to know Sam and discover the origins of the Songbird Cottage. This is the prequel to the rest of the Pleasant Bay series.

The Crystal Crescent Inn Boxed Set (Sambro Lighthouse Complete Series)

Amazon bestselling author Sylvia Price's Sambro Lighthouse Series, set on Canada's picturesque Crystal Crescent Beach, is a feel-good read perfect for fans of second chances with a bit of history and mystery all rolled into one. Enjoy all five sweet romance books in one collection for the first time!

Liz Beckett is grief-stricken when her beloved husband of thirty-five years dies after a long battle with cancer. Her daughter and best friend insist she needs a project to keep her occupied. Liz decides to share the beauty of Crystal Crescent Beach with those who visit the beautiful east coast of Nova Scotia and prepares to embark on the adventure of her life. She moves into the converted art studio at the bottom of her garden and turns the old family home into The Crystal Crescent Inn.

One of her first visitors is famous archeologist, Merc MacGill, and he's not there to admire the view. The handsome bachelor believes there's an undiscovered eighteenth-century farmstead hidden inside the creeks and coves of Crystal Crescent, and Liz wants to help him find it.

But it's not all smooth sailing at the inn that overlooks the historic Sambro Lighthouse. No one has realized it yet, but the lives of everyone in Liz's family are intertwined with those first settlers who landed in Nova Scotia over two hundred and fifty years ago. Will they be able to unravel the mystery? Will the lives of Liz's two children be changed forever if they discover the link between the lighthouse and their old home?

Take a trip to Crystal Crescent Beach and join Liz, her family, and guests as they navigate the storms and calm waters of life and love under the watchful eye of the lighthouse and its secret.

About the Author

Now an Amazon bestselling author, Sylvia Price is an author of Amish and contemporary romance and women's fiction. She especially loves writing uplifting stories about second chances!

Sylvia was inspired to write about the Amish as a result of the enduring legacy of Mennonite missionaries in her life. While living with them for three weeks, they got her a library card and encouraged her to start reading to cope with the loss of television and radio, giving Sylvia a newfound appreciation for books.

Although raised in the cosmopolitan city of

Montréal, Sylvia spent her adolescent and young adult years in Nova Scotia, and the beautiful countryside landscapes and ocean views serve as the backdrop to her contemporary novels.

After meeting and falling in love with an American while living abroad, Sylvia now resides in the US. She spends her days writing, hoping to inspire the next generation to read more stories. When she's not writing, Sylvia stays busy making sure her three young children are alive and well-fed.

Subscribe to Sylvia's newsletter at newsletter.sylviaprice.com to stay in the loop about new releases, freebies, promos, and more. As a thank-you, you will receive several FREE exclusive short stories that aren't available for purchase!

Learn more about Sylvia at amazon.com/author/sylviaprice and goodreads.com/sylviapriceauthor.

Follow Sylvia on Facebook at facebook.com/sylviapriceauthor for updates.

Join Sylvia's Advanced Reader Copies (ARC) team at arcteam.sylviaprice.com to get her books for free before they are released in exchange for honest reviews.

www.ingramcontent.com/pod-product-compliance
Lightning Source LLC
Chambersburg PA
CBHW030307160726
47992CB00005B/1915